GHOST OF SPIRIT BEAR

GHOST OF SPIRIT BEAR

BEN MIKAELSEN

SCHOLASTIC INC.
New York Toronto London Auckland
Sydney Mexico City New Delhi Hong Kong

ISBN 978-0-545-24354-4

12 11 10 9 8 7 6 5 4 3   10 11 12 13 14 15/0

Printed in the U.S.A.   40

First Scholastic printing, February 2010

Typography by Hilary Zarycky

This book is dedicated to all the readers
of *Touching Spirit Bear* who not only read the words
with their eyes, but felt the story with their hearts.

Every part of a Circle
Is both a beginning and an end.
And in a Circle
Everything is one.

PREFACE

(A REMOTE ISLAND IN SOUTHEAST ALASKA)

COLE MATTHEWS'S PAROLE officer, Garvey, met him at the cabin door carrying a crowbar.

"What's that for?" Cole asked, eyeing him.

"To tear down this cabin."

"You're not tearing down *my* cabin!" Cole challenged. "I built this thing."

"You're right, I'm not—*you* are," Garvey said, shoving the crowbar into Cole's hands, "the way *you* destroyed the first one that was built for you."

"You're never going to let me forget my mistakes, are you?" Cole said.

"I hope you never forget anything that happened out here on the island," Garvey answered. "You built this cabin to protect yourself. Has it done that?"

"Yeah, but maybe somebody else could use it."

"Building this cabin helped build your character," Garvey said. "Maybe the next person needs to build his character, too. It's your responsibility to leave this Earth the way you found it. You should know better than anybody that you are part of the Circle—if you diminish anything around you, you diminish yourself. Land needs to heal the same as people."

"How does tearing down a cabin heal the land?"

"This cabin isn't a part of nature like the trees and animals. Even without you, the world heals itself by rotting the wood floors and rusting the nails. Winds pry apart the walls, and eventually moss covers the roof."

"It's such a waste," Cole persisted.

"Only to you. The Earth wants back space where she can grow her grasses and feed her creatures again. Animals are afraid of this cabin."

"How about our totems?" Cole asked, pointing to the poles he and his friend Peter had planted on the shore above the high-tide line. The images they had carved during their isolation here on the island now faced proudly toward the ocean.

"The totems can stay—animals don't fear them."

Cole sighed. "Why can't we just burn the cabin?"

Garvey shook his head. "That causes pollution. It'll take years for the earth to grow back vegetation where you burned down the first cabin—you killed the microorganisms in the soil."

Reluctantly Cole pried a wall panel loose. It didn't do any good to argue with the Tlingit elder. Things were either right or wrong. Garvey thought everything in life affected everything else in the universe. To him, it was all about choices and consequences. You didn't pick your nose without it having some cosmic effect.

Cole glanced down the shoreline to where his friend Peter was loading the lantern, cooking gear, sleeping bags, and other provisions into the aluminum skiff.

"You built it, so you tear it down," Garvey said. "Don't be looking to Peter for help."

"I was just looking," Cole said.

Garvey pointed. "Anything that won't rot—plastic, glass, old shingles, tar paper—you'll take back to Drake and bury in the dump. Pull all the nails out and carry the planks deep into the forest, where they can once again become part of the land. By this time next year they will have rotted away. Mother Earth takes back quickly what's hers."

For two hours Cole worked. Peter and Garvey finished loading supplies, then sat on the rocks by the shoreline talking to each other. When the cabin was removed, Garvey walked over to the ground where it had stood and roughed up the dirt with a shovel. Then he spread leaves and pine needles over the disturbed soil. "Again this place has helped to heal," he said, closing his eyes. His lips moved silently. When he finished, he turned to Cole. "Take Peter upstream before we leave. I want you both to soak in the pond and carry the ancestor rocks one more time. It will need to last you a lifetime."

Cole called Peter to join him.

"I'm bringing the at.óow," Peter said, referring to the woven blanket Cole had given him. The handmade blanket with its bright red and blue totem images was the same blanket Garvey had given Cole to prove his trust when he first set foot on the island. Before that, it had been passed down through many generations of Tlingit elders.

With the at.óow wrapped around his shoulders, Peter followed Cole as they hiked along the stream. Every few steps, Peter stumbled. Once he fell but refused help getting back up. "You w-w-won't always be around to help me," he stuttered.

Cole slowed his walk.

When they reached the quiet pond, they took off their clothes and waded in without hesitation. No longer did the icy water take Cole's breath away—now he welcomed the piercing chill. Sitting on underwater rocks, he and Peter closed their eyes and breathed in. With each deep breath, Cole imagined himself becoming invisible, not to someone's sight, but quiet enough to fit into all that was around him—the landscape, the air, and the universe—a part of the Circle that Garvey always spoke of. Soon a squirrel chased another across a nearby stump. Fish swam within inches of Cole's legs, and birdcalls filled the air. These were things he never noticed when his mind was busy.

Cole allowed his thoughts to drift. The world was filled with different forces. Good ones—like animals, nature, and healing—had shaped him here. And then there was his old life back in Minnesota with his parents arguing every night. He remembered his father drinking and stomping around the house, a wild glare in his eyes, whiskey strong on his breath, and a belt hanging as a whip from his tight fist.

School hadn't been any better with all the bullies. The only way to survive was to fight back. Cole remembered drinking and trying drugs. His parents, who worked all the time, hadn't cared. They probably wouldn't have noticed if he had become an alien.

For excitement, Cole began stealing and getting into trouble with the law. One day, Peter Driscal had ratted on him for breaking into a hardware store, so Cole beat him up and smashed his head against the sidewalk. That brain injury now caused Peter to stutter, stumble, and walk leaning forward.

Cole's parents had refused to post bail when assault and robbery charges were filed. Even now, Cole wondered what would have happened if Garvey hadn't intervened. It was the Tlingit parole officer who had suggested an alternative called Circle Justice.

Instead of jail, Cole was offered a year's banishment on this remote Alaskan island. The isolation was to be a vision quest of sorts, a search into himself to try to rehabilitate his heart and soul. It was here that a white Spirit Bear had attacked and nearly killed him. It was here that he had angrily burned down the cabin that had been built for his survival. But it was also here that he had finally reached out and gently touched the Spirit Bear, finding beauty in life and finding his place in the Circle.

The year had been hard. After his recovery, Cole had been allowed to return to the island on one condition: he had to build another cabin himself and sell everything he owned to pay for the cost. That was why it had been so hard to tear down his small cabin this morning.

Cole breathed deeper and slowed his heartbeat as his thoughts drifted with the breeze that ruffled the pond. Gradually he forgot that he was a five feet, ten inch troubled teenager from Minneapolis. With each breath, he melted into the landscape around him. He felt no dimension, and he felt no more and no less important than the rock he sat on or the eagle that circled overhead. At moments like this, he knew what Garvey had meant when he had talked about being a part of the Circle. Cole felt himself drifting with the clouds, a part of the wind that rustled through the trees.

He didn't know how long he had soaked when he finally opened his eyes. He felt a presence and slowly turned his head. Not fifty feet away stood the big white Spirit Bear, staring at him, its thick coat of bushy hair shimmering in the breeze. The bear stood proudly, its eyes passive but aware.

Beside Cole, Peter already sat staring, mesmerized by the huge white creature. The bear must have sensed they were watching him. It turned and vanished effortlessly into the underbrush. "I'm going to miss seeing him," Peter whispered.

They sat in silence for a long moment before wading ashore. "Let's carry the ancestor rocks now," Cole murmured, as he dried himself and dressed. To speak out loud in the forests seemed disrespectful to nature.

Soon they finished dressing. They picked up the large ancestor rocks that they had carried so many times before.

Cole carried his with his left arm—his right arm was too weak from his injuries. As he climbed, he thought of the generations of ancestors who had gone before him to bring his life to where it was at this moment. He resolved to make his life count for something when he got back to Minneapolis so that the lives of his ancestors would not be wasted by his stupidity.

At the top of the hill, Cole and Peter set their stones on the ground and gave them a shove. As the rocks tumbled down the slope, Cole imagined all the frustrations and anger in his life rolling away. Then, in total silence, he followed Peter back to camp.

Garvey was waiting patiently for them beside the boat. "How did it go?" he asked.

"We s-s-saw the Spirit Bear," Peter stuttered.

"He came right to the pond," Cole added.

Garvey smiled. "That's good."

"It's kind of sad knowing we'll never see him again," Cole said.

"You'll always see him," Garvey said.

"Not in Minneapolis," Peter argued.

"Yes, you'll always find the Spirit Bear if you look."

CHAPTER 1

(TWO WEEKS LATER)
MINNEAPOLIS, MINNESOTA

WALKING TO SCHOOL the first morning was strange and different. On the island, Cole had hiked the rocky path to the pond each morning at daybreak. Around him had been the sounds of seagulls calling, the screech of owls, and twigs snapping in the underbrush. The pungent smell of pine trees, salt water, and rotting seaweed had filled the air. Sometimes the chuffing sound of killer whales broke the stillness as they breached. And always Cole had felt the hidden eyes of the Spirit Bear calmly watching him from deep in the trees.

Here, walking on a smooth sidewalk in the city, Cole smelled car exhaust. He heard dogs barking, a garbage truck loading trash, and the traffic going by. A siren screamed in the distance. He missed the Spirit Bear. The city felt like some foreign planet. Cole wanted to cover his ears and close his eyes to it all. He didn't fit into this world.

Cole noticed his reflection in the window of a parked

car as he walked. He had grown taller and thinner on the island. His skin was weathered and rough, and his muscles had become strong and lean. His old clothes no longer fit him, but he felt uncomfortable in his new ones.

As he neared the school, Cole hugged his injured right arm against his waist and tried not to limp. If he let the arm hang, it swung awkwardly because of the bone and muscle damage. He dared not let his injuries show. Around the bullies, he'd be like a wounded rabbit with wolves.

Cole blinked back his feelings of fear and frustration. On the island he had learned to control his emotions. He had learned from Garvey and another Tlingit elder, Edwin, that he could never fully get rid of anger because it was a memory. But he had also learned to focus on the good. A good day wasn't a day without clouds but rather a day when one focused on finding the sunlight behind the clouds.

Cole wondered if he could keep that same focus back here in the city. The very moment he stepped onto the plane heading for Minneapolis that concern had begun eating at his gut. What would happen when the island was simply a memory and the Spirit Bear was only a ghost from his past? What would happen when he returned to the bullies and gangs? The students would remember only the old angry Cole who once prowled the hallways looking for fights. And maybe that old angry Cole still existed, a monster who would one day return without warning.

As he approached the school, the knot tightened in Cole's throat and kept him from swallowing. A statue of the

Minneapolis Central bulldog mascot seemed to snarl at him from its familiar pedestal on the front lawn. The dog had one leg broken off and one ear missing. Cole remembered spraying graffiti on the marble pedestal himself. Now it was tagged with gang symbols, some that Cole no longer recognized. Looking at the ratty bulldog made his memory of the proud and magical white Spirit Bear seem like a distant dream.

Groups of kids hung around outside the school, shoving and slapping at one another and shouting names. Most wore baggy pants and T-shirts. Some wore bandannas or jackets with gang colors. Already candy wrappers and soda cans littered the lawn.

Cole recognized some of the kids, but they seemed like strangers. The cliques and gangs had already begun gathering: the preppies, the jocks, the Goths, the red groups and blue groups, blacks, Asians, Hispanics, and a dozen more. Each group eyed the others with disdain and distrust.

Cole felt like he was outside a fishbowl looking in. None of it made sense anymore. He had been fifteen and in tenth grade when he had beaten up Peter. Now he was coming back at seventeen but only starting eleventh grade because of the classes he'd missed. He felt a lifetime older.

Cole noticed one plain-looking white girl with long straight brown hair approaching the school.

"Hey, slut!" shouted a girl sitting on the steps near the door.

The girl kept walking, looking down at the sidewalk.

"Look who's calling who a slut!" shouted one of the jocks.

"Shut up, jack—!" the girl yelled back.

"Shut up yourself, b—!" the boy answered.

Suddenly Cole wanted to scream, Stop it! Everybody just shut up! Garvey's words came back to him: "Diminish anything around you and you diminish yourself." Did these kids know they were destroying themselves with every word?

Students who recognized Cole turned and stared openly. His pulse quickened and his face warmed when he heard their whispers. In the past, he would have challenged any kid who dared to stare. Now he drew in a deep breath and lowered his eyes, afraid of what he might do if confronted.

A familiar voice interrupted Cole's thoughts. "Hey, you," Peter called, hurrying over in his stumbling gait. "H-h-how are ya?"

"Good. How are you doing?"

The smile left Peter's face. "Two kids have called me a retard already. I wish we were still on the island. I want to go back and soak in the pond."

Cole studied his friend's troubled face. The beating and the brain injury had left Peter superemotional. Sometimes he laughed and cried at the same time. Cole remembered Peter's first nights on the island, waking up screaming as if he were still being attacked. With time, his fears had calmed, but Cole worried that those haunted thoughts would return here in the city.

Cole knew he was responsible for Peter's injuries, but he also knew he had helped him. After Peter attempted suicide the second time, Cole had suggested that the fearful boy visit the island. He wanted to show Peter that the monster he feared no longer existed.

At first, Peter's parents had refused, but in desperation they finally agreed under the condition that Garvey accompany the two boys to help protect their son.

On the island, Cole had struggled hard to help Peter discover that he, too, was a part of something much larger than himself, like a strand woven into a blanket or a brushstroke in a picture. Peter learned to be aware of but not to focus on his own self.

Standing now on the school grounds watching the other students, emotions welled up in Cole. A thought kept haunting him: Maybe the monster that Peter once feared still existed.

In each class, Cole picked a desk near the back, trying not to be noticed. During lunch, he sat alone, eating slowly, chewing, tasting, and appreciating each mouthful before he swallowed. Kids around him stuffed food into their faces, arguing and complaining.

"These hamburgers suck!" one girl grumbled.

"So do the french fries," another student added.

Cole watched kids dump tray after tray of half-eaten food into the garbage can. He wondered how everybody would behave if they had almost starved on an island. What if they had been forced to eat vomit, insects, and mice just to stay alive, as he had? What if they, too, had touched the Spirit Bear?

An assembly was called for the last period. Cole couldn't find Peter, so he sat alone in the bleachers, ignoring the shouting and shoving. The teachers bunched together against the wall under the mural of the vicious bulldog mascot. They visited with one another and ignored the students.

On the gym floor, a short, neatly dressed woman stepped up to the podium and tapped the microphone. "Okay, listen up everyone! I'm Ms. Kennedy, the new principal," she said in a monotone, as if her voice were a recording.

"Hey, witch, you listen up!" a student screamed back.

The woman pulled the microphone closer. "Welcome! I'm Ms. Kennedy, your new principal. I've called this assembly to welcome you back to Minneapolis Central High, home of the proud Bulldogs. I appreciate your being here."

"What choice do we have?" another student shouted.

The principal droned on over the shouting and laughter. When the assembly finally ended, Cole braced himself for more shoving. A student shouted, "The b— won't last a week!"

They were probably right, Cole thought. He spotted Peter leaving school through a side door and ran to catch up. "Hey, what did you think of the new principal?" he asked.

"I th-th-think she'll get munched for lunch."

Cole nodded his agreement. "How was your first day?"

Peter stared at the sidewalk without answering.

"Did more kids trash you?"

Peter shrugged. "It's no big deal. How 'bout you?"

Cole pretended to be the announcer at a circus. "Come one, come all," he shouted. "See the freak boy who was attacked by a bear!"

Peter laughed and chimed in, "See the boy who got his head smashed and had to go to Alaska so he wouldn't commit suicide."

Cole spoke bitterly. "We're both in trouble when everybody figures out that fighting will send me to jail."

Peter wrinkled his forehead. "We have to think like we did on the island or we'll both be back where we started. I wish we were soaking in the pond right now. We wouldn't have all these problems."

"I'll figure out something," Cole said.

"If you find a pond, maybe I can figure out how to carry ancestor rocks," Peter said, looking at his watch. "Hey, I gotta get home."

Cole watched his friend limp away and then headed for home himself. His mother now worked as an office manager for a trucking company and wouldn't get off work for a couple of hours, so Cole took his time.

He had walked several blocks when he found himself passing Frazier's grocery store. Suddenly an idea popped into his head. He used to shop at this store with his mother. Once she had asked the checkout person if they could buy a case of frozen hamburgers for a picnic she was planning with Dad. The man had led them back into a large walk-in freezer where they stored frozen goods. Cole remembered seeing his breath and shivering. That freezer would be cold like the stream.

Cole hesitated, then walked inside and asked a tall woman working behind the meat counter, "Can I speak with the manager?"

"I'm Betty. I manage the dairy and meat department," the lady said, wiping her hands on a white apron. "Can I help you?"

"I have a weird question."

"Well, maybe I have a weird answer."

"I was sent up to Alaska to stay on an island for a year."

"I read about you somewhere," she said. "Didn't you end up spending time with the boy you attacked?"

Cole nodded. "We went every morning and soaked in an ice-cold pond to help us clear away our angry thoughts." He picked nervously at a fingernail. "Here we don't have a pond anymore. Could we come and try sitting in your freezer?"

The lady laughed with surprise. "You really want to come and just sit in the freezer to get cold?"

Cole smiled nervously. "Long enough to clear our minds so we're not angry."

"You'll freeze your britches," she joked. Then she studied Cole. "You're serious, aren't you?"

"We have to find something like the pond to keep us from getting mad again."

"Why don't you just decide to be happy?"

"It's not that easy—please."

Betty frowned. "This isn't something I want to adver-
tise. Would you come in before school?"

Cole nodded.

"Okay. I'll put a couple of plastic chairs back there and
let you try it."

Cole reached over the counter and shook her hand.
"Thanks so much. Thanks a million."

Cole couldn't wait to tell Peter his idea, so he hiked the
six blocks to Peter's house. Hopefully Mr. and Mrs. Driscal
weren't home—they still didn't like seeing him with Peter.
Nervously, he knocked.

"Wh-wh-what are you doing here?" Peter asked when
he opened the door, glancing over his shoulder.

"Who is it, honey?" called Mrs. Driscal, walking from
the kitchen with a towel in her hand. Her smile faded
when she spotted Cole. "Can we help you?" she asked, her
voice suddenly guarded.

"I know you don't want Peter hanging around me,
Mrs. Driscal," Cole said hesitantly, "but we're friends now.
I'm not going to hurt him."

"You've already done that," she said.

"What are you doing here?" Peter asked again.

Cole told Mrs. Driscal how he and Peter wanted to
soak and carry ancestor rocks again. Deliberately he
explained his plan. "Sitting in the freezer would be kind of
like soaking in the pond," he concluded. "Can Peter come
with me tomorrow morning?"

Mrs. Driscal hesitated. "We'll have to discuss this with
Peter's father."

"Mom, y-y-you know Dad will say no," Peter said, "but he's not always right!"

"Let's just forget it," Cole said. "I'll see you in school tomorrow."

"No! I'll go to the freezer with you," Peter said stubbornly. He turned to his mother. "Mom, I'm standing up for myself—you said yourself that was good. Besides, I have an idea, too, how we can carry ancestor rocks like on the island."

"And what's that?" she asked.

"I'll tell you if it works. Cole, do you want to go right now and see *my* idea?"

Mrs. Driscal threw her hands up. "Oh, so now you don't even tell me what you're doing?"

Peter started down the driveway.

"We *will* discuss this with your father later," Mrs. Driscal called.

"Where are you going?" Cole asked, as they turned onto the sidewalk.

"First, to the Salvation Army store."

"The Salvation Army?"

"Yeah, we have to get our ancestor rocks." A sly smile parted Peter's lips.

Curious, Cole followed, walking slowly to match Peter's struggling gait. By the time they reached the Salvation Army store, Peter was nearly exploding with impatience. "Aren't you going to ask me what we're using for ancestor rocks?" he said.

Cole smiled. "You'll tell me when you want to."

"Bowling balls," Peter announced, barging through the front door. "They have a whole mess of bowling balls in the back. Some of the chipped ones are only a dollar."

Cole followed Peter to where a dozen bowling balls had been set against a wall. "But there are no hills around here to climb," he said.

Peter picked up a ball and headed for the checkout counter. "Wanna bet?" he said.

CHAPTER 2

COLE CARRIED HIS bowling ball awkwardly from the store and followed Peter. He felt shame each time Peter stumbled. It was no wonder that Mr. and Mrs. Driscal still thought of him as some kind of monster.

Peter didn't slow until they reached an old abandoned apartment building on a back street. Condemned and Keep Out notices hung on the outside walls. "This is our mountain," Peter declared, entering between the front doors that hung broken and twisted.

"The signs say 'Keep Out,'" Cole said, following reluctantly.

"That's just for people without bowling balls," Peter said with a laugh.

"What if we get caught? That could get me in big trouble with Garvey."

"Caught for what?" Peter said as he crossed the lobby to the stairwell. "Carrying bowling balls into an old building? We're not robbers or terrorists."

"No, we're crazy!"

"Better crazy than lazy," Peter said. He glanced down into the dark basement. "I wonder what's down there."

"I'm not finding out," Cole said.

"Maybe some other day," Peter said, starting up the stairwell.

"How many floors are there?" Cole asked, adjusting the heavy ball in his good arm.

"I counted ten from the outside," Peter said, leading the way.

As they climbed the dark and musty stairwell, eerie shadows like ghosts fell on the walls. Finally, sweating, they reached the top landing. It was covered with broken glass. Cole glanced back down the stairs. "We didn't take much time to think about our ancestors coming up."

"We'll do that tomorrow," Peter promised. "Let's roll our anger away now and get out of here."

Cole hesitated. "If we roll these balls down the steps, it's gonna wreck something."

"You can't wreck an old building that's already wrecked," Peter argued. "What do you want to do—drop them out the window instead?"

"That's even worse—what if we hit someone?"

"You chicken," Peter said, walking over to a broken window. "It's just an empty lot—nobody's down there."

"Man, the balls will be going about a million miles an hour when they hit."

"That's the cool part." Peter grinned. With a grunt, he

hefted his ball out the window. Cole ran to Peter's side in time to see the ball hit the ground with a dull thud. "It actually bounced." Peter laughed. "Your turn."

"You're certified nuts," Cole said, shoving his own ball out the window. "Let's get out of here." Quickly he turned and rushed down the stairs, not waiting to watch his ball hit.

As he ran out the front door, Cole half expected to see police cars waiting for them.

"Let's go get the balls," Peter said, heading around the building.

Cole followed, surprised to find the bowling balls had not broken apart. Depressions in the hard ground marked where each had landed. Cole picked up his ball and headed for the street. "I'm getting out of here," he said.

"Let's just leave the balls here," Peter said. "Why carry them back and forth each day?"

Reluctantly, Cole agreed to go back inside where they set the bowling balls under the stairwell.

"Okay, now let's get out of here," Cole said. "This place gives me the creeps."

"Tomorrow we'll think about our ancestors and close our eyes to imagine our anger falling away," Peter said as they walked toward home. "So, what time do you want to meet at the grocery store in the morning?"

"School starts at eight, so maybe about seven. Will that be okay with your dad?"

"Nothing's okay with him." Suddenly, Peter pointed. "Hey, look!"

Half a block ahead, Cole saw a flash of white disappear

around the side of a building. He glanced at Peter in astonishment. "It looked like a Spirit Bear."

Peter nodded in disbelief.

Both boys broke into a run. In seconds they rounded the corner, but all they found was an old homeless man, standing beside a shopping cart stacked with junk. His beard was choppy as if it had been trimmed with a knife, and even in the warm fall air, he had a ragged white blanket draped over his shoulders. As they watched, the old bum pulled out a piece of wood and began whittling.

Suddenly he glanced up and caught them staring. Quickly Cole and Peter retreated around the corner, then stopped and broke up laughing. "Jeez! It was just some tramp with a white blanket." Peter chuckled. "How could we have thought it was a Spirit Bear?"

"Being in Alaska froze our brains."

"I better get home," Peter said. "I'll see you in the morning." He hesitated. "Hey, Cole."

"What?"

"It's fun being your friend."

Later, when his mother got home from work, Cole told her about his plan to sit in the freezer each morning. "The lady said we could try it and see if it works."

She looked at him dubiously. "Can't you get rid of your anger without sitting in a freezer? How do other people do it?"

"Lots of people don't."

She hesitated as if struggling with her own thoughts.

"Just make sure you're no trouble to anyone."

"It'll be okay," Cole assured her. Seeing the doubt in her eyes, he decided not to tell her yet about dropping bowling balls out of the abandoned building. She'd really have kittens over that one. He changed the subject. "Where does Dad live now?"

"Across town, closer to his job." She took a broom out of the closet, avoiding Cole's gaze. "Why?"

Cole shrugged. "Just wondering. He never even came to the airport to say good-bye when I left. Is he still mad at me?"

"I have no idea what your father thinks anymore," she said, slamming the closet door.

"Is the divorce final?"

"It's been final for months now," she said, starting to sweep. "I won't stop you from seeing your father if that's what you want. But I don't want to see him myself. He's no longer the man I married twenty years ago."

"None of us are what we used to be," Cole said, following his mother as she moved through the house, cleaning. Each room flooded Cole's mind with memories and emotions. The laundry room was where his father had turned the belt around and hit him with the buckle end for the first time. But it was also where they once played hide-and-seek.

His mother finally set down the broom. "Are you hungry?" she asked. "You look like a scarecrow—you'd have trouble getting wet in a shower."

"It wasn't like we didn't have plenty to eat on the

island," Cole explained. "Eating just wasn't important."

"Maybe I need to go to an island," she joked, patting her hips. "Why don't I fix us a couple of hot dogs."

Cole walked ahead of her back into the kitchen. "Let me—I want to show you something."

Curious, she agreed.

Cole did not speak until the hot dogs had finished boiling. As he took them out of the water, he explained, "All of life is like these hot dogs. If we cook them simply to stay alive, then that is what happens. If we treat them special and share them, they become a celebration and a feast."

"Did Garvey teach you that?"

Cole nodded, sprinkling each hot dog with cheese and garnishing them with diced tomatoes and pepper. As an afterthought, he lit a candle on the table.

His mother took a bite and chewed with a smile. For the first time Cole could remember, he saw pride and respect in her eyes. "You really did change on the island, didn't you?" she said.

"Yes, I did. But I don't want you to believe me because I say so. I want you to believe me because now my actions prove it."

"You're my son," she said quietly. "I believe you because I love you."

Cole had never liked being touched, but he leaned over and hugged his mother hard.

Cole awoke before his alarm sounded the next morning. After a quick breakfast, he headed out. At the grocery store, he met Peter coming from the opposite direction. "Must have been okay with your dad," Cole said.

"He acted like I was trying to do something wrong."

"He's probably just mad at *me*."

"It's more than that," Peter answered.

"What do you mean?"

"Even before you beat me up, he used to blame me for everything. I never did anything right. Now I *really* don't make him happy."

"Why is that?"

"'Cause now I *can't* do anything right."

"You do a lot of things right," Cole said as they entered the grocery store.

"You boys are here plenty early. I just got here myself," Betty, the dairy manager, said, greeting them.

"You sure this is okay?" Cole asked.

"Hey, nobody else is waiting to sit in the freezer. Don't give me a chance to change my mind."

The door to the cold room was heavy, with brass handles like a bank vault's. The handles allowed the door to be opened from both sides. Cole and Peter sat on the plastic chairs, crowded between pallets of shrimp and frozen strawberries. Cole closed his eyes and tried to pretend he was soaking in a cold pond. He peeked and caught Peter peeking back. Breathing in deeply, Cole closed his eyes again and imagined icy water. The freezer air felt good on his skin. He pretended his mind was a calm pond with no waves, but no matter how hard he tried, thoughts of his father left ripples.

Fifteen minutes later, Cole stood stiffly, walked to the door, and pulled on the big brass handle to let himself out. He guessed that Peter would stay a little longer to prove that leaving was his idea. That was what he had often done in Alaska. He would eat an hour after Cole to prove he wasn't hungry when he was really starved. Or he would stay up late, reading and fighting sleep with the lantern on to prove he wasn't tired after a long hike. More than once, Cole had taken a book from Peter's hands and turned off the lantern when he'd found his friend asleep.

Cole waited outside the freezer until the big door swung open and Peter came out shivering. "We must really be happy now!" Peter said.

"That was tropical compared to the pond," Cole joked. "I almost got heat stroke."

"Yeah," Peter said, rubbing his red arms. "This is sunburn. I was sweating the whole time."

"Thanks," Cole called to Betty as they left. "We'll see you tomorrow."

"Okay," she answered with a wave. "I hope you two have a happy day. Maybe we would have world peace if we put all the world leaders in a big freezer each morning."

"Maybe," Cole allowed.

As they walked the half mile to school, Peter seemed lost in thought. "Do you really think dropping bowling balls and sitting in a freezer will help us?" he asked suddenly.

"I don't know. Maybe we should carve totems again or try dancing like on the island."

"We could just go to a school dance."

Cole shook his head. "That's not the same."

Peter agreed. "If we danced here like we did on the island, they'd think we were crazy. Remember how you used to run around with your arms out like an eagle?"

"That wasn't as funny as when you used to jump straight up with your chest out like a breaching whale."

"At least we danced to show what we had learned from the animals," Peter said. "Here they just dance to act cool."

Cole and Peter were still talking about the island as they reached the front lawn of the school. Suddenly a loud voice behind them shouted, "Hey, look, it's the psycho and the gimp!"

Cole turned as a gang of five boys approached. He recognized several of them.

"They were the ones who hassled me yesterday," Peter whispered.

Keith, the one leading the rest, was a big kid. Cole remembered kicking his butt in a fight two years earlier.

"Wh-wh-why don't you guys just leave us alone," Peter said.

"Wh-wh-why don't you just shut your face, retard," Keith said, giving Peter a shove. "We don't like gimps."

Fear showed in Peter's eyes, and Cole stepped forward. "We haven't done anything to you. Leave Peter alone," he said, his hands tightening into fists.

"Oh, so now you're telling us what to do," said Eddy, a shorter boy with tight curly hair. "Bad mistake." Eddy shoved Peter and sent him sprawling to the ground.

Cole's heart pounded fast and his face felt hot. He tried to stay calm, but nothing could control what he was feeling. All his life he had been made to feel helpless. Now, seeing the bullies hurt his defenseless friend, Cole's anger exploded. "Your mistake, Eddy," he said, giving the boy a sudden shove that knocked him to the ground beside Peter.

"Don't fight!" Peter screamed. "Let them beat me up!"

Keith turned and punched Cole hard in the stomach.

Cole swung back viciously with all his might, catching Keith's face. As he swung a second time, a shrill whistle sounded. The football coach came running across the lawn. "Every one of you to the principal's office," he shouted.

At first nobody moved.

"Now!" the coach bellowed.

As Cole helped Peter to his feet, he turned. "Coach," he pleaded. "I was only trying to—"

"Save your excuses!" the coach snapped.

CHAPTER 3

COLE AND PETER waited anxiously with Keith and his friends in the main office.

"You guys squeal on us, you're roadkill," Keith said.

Cole and Peter ignored him.

Ten minutes passed before the principal walked in. "So what happened?" she asked, handing some paperwork to the secretary.

"Nuthin'," Keith said. "We were just minding our business and these two started calling us names. They came over and shoved us—we were just defending ourselves."

The principal turned to Cole and Peter. "Is that what happened?"

Keith shot Peter a menacing look.

Trembling, Peter nodded.

"Is that what happened?" she asked again, looking at Cole.

Cole hung his head, refusing to answer. Nothing he said would help. This lady, with her lipstick, fingernail polish, and heels, would never understand.

The principal examined all seven of them. "You five go wait in my office," she said to Keith and his gang. "I'll speak to you in a few minutes. Peter, I want you to go to class." When the rest had left, she motioned Cole into a side room. "You wait there while I call your parole officer."

"But I didn't start the fight," Cole pleaded.

"It takes two to fight."

"Like I had a choice," Cole said in desperation. "If I screw up even once, I go to jail."

She looked at him sharply. "Well, you just screwed up," she said, walking toward her office.

Cole entered the room and slumped into a chair, smoldering with anger. Inside he felt the monster raging—the one who had hurt Peter. Now it wanted to break something or hurt somebody. This hadn't been his fault!

It was nearly an hour before Garvey arrived. He entered the small room where Cole sat waiting and stared at him for a long moment before he spoke. "Stupid, stupid, stupid!" he said. "Why did you allow this?"

"I didn't allow anything!" Cole said angrily. "I was—"

"Save it," Garvey snapped.

"Don't you even want to know what happened?"

"Exactly what you let happen," Garvey said.

Cole clenched his fists. "You don't get it, do you? I didn't start anything."

"Why are you afraid of other people?" Garvey asked.

"I'm not!" Cole snapped. "I don't care if those creeps beat me up. I'm here because they picked on Peter."

Garvey shook his head. "No, you're here because of how you reacted to them picking on Peter."

"What's the difference?"

Garvey pulled up a chair across from Cole. His voice became deliberate. "The bullies picking on you this morning is something that happened outside your body."

"Uh, duh, brilliant, Einstein."

Garvey ignored him. "You can't control things outside your body, so don't try. You learned that on the island."

"So what should I have done this morning?"

"Control *your* reality—what happens *inside* your body. I'm talking about how you react. That's real control." Garvey studied Cole as if he were a puzzle. "Ever notice that if you walk into a grocery store happy, everyone else seems happy?" he said. "If you go in mad, everybody seems mad, and yet it's the same people."

"I don't see what you're getting at. This isn't a grocery store. Those jerks won't be nice if I smile at them."

"Okay, let's try again. If a semi truck roars past you on the highway, is that *your* reality?"

"I suppose," Cole allowed.

"No!" Garvey challenged. "If you choose to step in front of that semi, you create one ugly reality for yourself. If you choose to wave to the driver, that creates a whole different reality. Either way the truck just passed by you. How you react creates your real reality. You're not here this morning because of what some bully did. You're here because of how you reacted to the bullies."

"Don't you see, I *didn't* have any choice," Cole insisted.

"By fighting back, you gave them the control and power they wanted." Garvey stood. "Stand up. I want to show you something."

When Cole rose, Garvey shoved him back into his chair. "I'm pretty strong, aren't I?" he said, smiling.

"You just surprised me."

"Okay, stand up again."

Hesitantly, Cole stood.

"Are you stronger than me?" Garvey challenged.

Cole shrugged.

"Let's find out. Go ahead, push me."

"I'm not going to hurt you," Cole said.

"Believe me, you won't hurt me," Garvey said. "I've raised two teenage daughters. Go ahead, shove me."

Cole shoved. When he did, Garvey backed up and Cole hardly touched him.

"That was lame," Garvey taunted. "Shove like a man."

Angrily, Cole shoved harder. Again Garvey backed away, only this time he put out a foot and tripped Cole. At the same time he jerked on Cole's arm, sending him sprawling to the floor.

"Why did you do that?" Cole demanded, scrambling to his feet.

"You tell me," Garvey said. "You're this strong macho guy who says he's going to protect Peter. Shoot, you can't even protect yourself. Look who ended up on the floor. Don't you see, when I shoved you, you resisted me, which made me strong."

"So what's your point?"

"When you shoved me, I backed away from you, which took away your strength and threw you off balance. I could never have tripped you if you hadn't tried to shove me first. I used your strength to beat you."

Cole stared sullenly at Garvey as he sat down.

Garvey shook his head. "You know better than anyone that kids like Keith are the most insecure students in school. I didn't make that up—that's just a simple fact. They're not stronger than you."

Cole rubbed at his neck. "So tell me exactly what I should have done this morning. I have to protect Peter, but if I fight again, the Circle won't give me another chance."

"The Circle doesn't mind you fighting, but don't use your fists."

"I can't just sit down on the ground."

Garvey shrugged. "Actually, sitting on the ground might have helped. What satisfaction would you get from kicking or beating up somebody who's not fighting back? My guess is you wouldn't be here right now."

"No, I'd be in the nurse's office," Cole said. "You're dead wrong. I always used to beat up kids who wouldn't fight back."

"When the bear attacked you, did you fight back?"

Cole nodded.

"Did it help?"

Cole shook his head, remembering how fighting back had only angered the big creature.

/ 33 /

"When did the Spirit Bear let you touch him?"

"When I was gentle. But here nobody trusts me."

"Trust has to be earned one person at a time, one day at a time. You've changed, but you have to decide what you're going to do around people who haven't changed."

"It's hard without the pond, the totems, and our ancestor rocks. I feel helpless."

The weathered creases on Garvey's face looked chiseled as he pointed to his head. "The real ponds, totems, and ancestor rocks are up here now. You have total control."

Cole gave up arguing. "So what happens now?"

"Thursday evening the Circle meets with you again," Garvey said, referring to the community members who had originally decided Cole's fate when he applied for Circle Justice before going to the island. "Now they'll decide if your banishment worked."

"Will I go to jail for what happened today?" Cole asked.

Garvey shrugged. "It depends. You had it easy on the island with nobody in your face." Garvey rapped his fingers on the table. "I went through banishment at your age and thought it was successful until I returned home. And then everything went to hell. I wasn't strong enough to keep the peace I found on the island. Surviving up there turned out to be the easiest part."

"Why were you sent to the island?"

Garvey didn't answer. He looked at his watch. "Hey, I have to go. I'll talk to your principal about this morning, and I'll see you at Circle on Thursday evening."

"Does my dad know about the meeting?"

"I called him—he said he was too busy."

"Sounds like Dad."

Garvey looked Cole straight in the eyes. "I'm pretending this morning never happened," he said. "It better not happen again."

But Cole knew it *would* happen again. People like Keith didn't just stop being jerks.

At lunch, Keith passed behind Cole as he sat eating. "You're dead meat!" he whispered.

Two tables away, Cole recognized the thin, brown-haired girl who had been called a slut the morning before. She sat with her head lowered, trying to ignore two girls who crowded her from both sides, laughing as they grabbed french fries from her plate. Without thinking, Cole walked over. "Knock it off!" he said.

The girls moved away, making snide faces.

The thin girl looked up at him fearfully.

"Those girls are jerks," Cole said.

"So are the idiots that picked on you this morning," she said.

"Did you see that?" Cole asked, sitting down.

She nodded. "Why were they picking on you?"

"I guess I kind of have a reputation. How about you—why were those girls picking on you?"

"They don't need a reason."

A loud bell signaled the end of the school day. Cole met Peter outside, glad the second day of school had ended.

"Hey, what happened after I left this morning?" Peter asked.

"The principal called Garvey."

"Was he mad?"

"He wasn't happy," Cole said. "How was your day?"

"I kept getting shoved in the hallway. Every time Eddy saw me, he knocked the books out of my hands."

"Keith told me I was dead meat."

Peter grew thoughtful. "This sounds funny, but I think I w-w-was a little to blame for you beating me up."

"What are you talking about?"

"I was a doormat," Peter said. "I always let people walk on me."

"But you stand up for yourself more than you used to," Cole said, remembering Peter defying his mother and father.

"That's true," Peter said. "Hey, are you up for carrying our ancestor rocks again?"

Cole hesitated. "Isn't there a better way?"

"Are you scared?"

"I'm scared of getting in trouble before the Circle meets," Cole said. "But if you really want to, okay."

It was a quick walk to the abandoned building. Cole paused outside. "Hey, Peter, when we carry the bowling balls today, we have to think more about our ancestors and about our past."

Peter agreed. "And we have to pretend we're dropping our anger away."

Glancing around, they slipped inside and waited for

their eyes to adjust to the dim light. Then they crossed the lobby to the stairwell where they had left the bowling balls. "Where are they?" Cole said, glancing around.

Peter checked under the steps. "Somebody took them."

"Who would steal something like that?"

"Nobody even knew they were here." Peter peered down the darkened stairwell that led to the basement. "Maybe they're down there."

"I'm not going there to look!" Cole exclaimed.

"You big chicken," Peter said, starting down.

"I'm a big *live* chicken," Cole said. "Don't be crazy!"

Peter paused to listen. "Th-th-there's nobody here."

"Then why are you going so slow?"

"It's dark—I don't want to trip." Peter descended cautiously into the darkness.

"I don't like this!" Cole called down.

"I found them," Peter called back, returning up the stairs with his bowling ball. "They were on the bottom step."

"Where's mine?"

"Go get your own."

Cole tiptoed down, grabbed his ball, and rushed back up. "This place really gives me the creeps—I'm out of here."

"I think we should still carry our ancestor rocks," Peter said stubbornly.

"And what if some mass murderer is hiding upstairs waiting to attack us?" Cole tried to sound like he was kidding.

Peter headed up the stairs on his own. "W-w-wait here if you don't dare."

Reluctantly Cole followed. "Don't forget to think about your ancestors."

As he climbed, Cole reminded himself of all the generations of people who had lived and died before him to create his life. Just as he had on the island, he thought of the events that made him who he had become, the beatings by his father, all the fights at school, the arrests, the Circle meetings, going to the island, the mauling, discovering beauty and forgiveness, and now being here with Peter. And then Cole thought about his own future. He still hadn't seen or heard anything from his father.

Floor by floor they worked their way up. Suddenly Peter stopped. "I heard something."

Cole paused. "It's your imagination," he said, passing Peter on the stairs. "Now who's chicken?" He led the rest of the way to the top. "Okay, let's drop these things and get out of here."

Carefully Peter balanced his ball in the broken window. "We have to remember we're getting rid of our anger," he said, then shoved hard.

Cole looked out in time to see the impact, and then he gave his own ball a heave. As he watched it plummet down, his anger at Keith still smoldered.

CHAPTER 4

COLE AND PETER circled quickly down the steps, floor after floor, until they reached the lobby. Peter headed straight for the broken doors, but Cole stopped him with a loud whisper, "Hey, Peter, look!"

A grocery cart piled high with junk was parked in the hallway. "Isn't that the cart the old homeless guy was pushing?" Peter whispered.

"It wasn't here when we came in," Cole said. "He must live in the basement!"

"I told you I heard something."

Both boys rushed from the building and across the overgrown lawn toward the street. "Forget the bowling balls," Cole said.

"Do you think he lives there?" Peter asked, hobbling.

"It's probably where he stores his victims."

"Quit it! I'm being serious."

When they reached a stoplight and paused to catch

their breaths, Peter said, "Cole, maybe that old g-g-guy is scared of us, too."

"We haven't done anything to him."

"He hasn't hurt us either. I wonder what happened to make him homeless?"

"Who knows. What happened to make Keith a bully?" Cole said.

"If we run into those guys again, you should just run," Peter said. "Then only one of us gets beat up."

"That's dumb," Cole said sharply. "We're friends, aren't we?"

Peter scratched his chin in thought and then broke into a smile. "I think I have a secret weapon."

"It's not a gun or a knife, is it?" Cole asked.

"No, I'll bring my cell phone to school."

"So you can call the ambulance after we get beat up?"

"Don't be a jerk. Listen—we're not allowed to use cell phones in school, but it's not illegal to *carry* them. I'll get the principal's number somewhere, then I'll program it in so all I have to do is push the Send button and it will dial automatically. I won't even have to take the phone out of my pocket. I have one of those little microphones that I'll clip inside my shirt. If we get attacked, I'll reach in my pocket and push the button. The principal will hear everything that happens."

"I don't think it'll work," Cole said.

"You have a better idea?"

Cole had to admit that he didn't.

★ ★ ★

Wednesday morning, Cole struggled with his thoughts and emotions as he sat in the freezer. What if his time on the island had been a waste? Every day his anger seemed to come back stronger. What if he *was* nothing more than a big screwup?

Peter stood and opened the freezer door. "I'm about done," he said casually, trying not to show his shivering.

Cole followed him out.

Betty was whistling merrily as they walked from the back of the grocery store. She waved to them. "So are you both happy now?" she called.

"It's not something that happens overnight," Cole said, irritated by her cheerfulness.

Peter seemed annoyed, too. "How come you're always happy?" he asked suddenly, stopping at the counter. "You must not have much bad stuff in your life."

Betty allowed a sad smile. "I've had plenty of bad things in my life," she said. "I'm not always happy. But would it make things better if I let myself get down all the time?"

Cole walked to the counter beside Peter. "It's not that easy—you can't just decide not to be mad."

"Says who?" she asked.

"I spent more than a year on an island figuring out how not to be mad all the time."

"Maybe you're a slow learner," she kidded with an easy laugh. "Mostly I sort things out raising my plants. Ever try growing orchids?"

The boys shook their heads.

"I suspect there's really only one way to find happiness."

"What's that?" Peter asked.

"You have to *want* to be happy—some people don't."

Because they were in different classes, Cole didn't see Peter again until after school.

"The secret weapon is locked and loaded," Peter announced when they met. He patted the cell phone in his pocket and opened a button to show off the little microphone hidden inside his shirt. "I found the principal's cell number on my science teacher's desk."

"Have you told the principal about your idea?"

"Maybe that w-w-wouldn't be smart."

Cole smiled. The idea was crazy, but at least it gave Peter a sense of confidence.

As they left the school grounds together, they passed the bulldog statue. "I hate that thing," Cole said.

Peter agreed. "Everywhere you look at school there's a picture of that ugly mutt."

"Hey, I've been thinking," Peter continued. "You're right. It's not smart dropping the bowling balls. It's going to get us in trouble if we get caught. Besides, I'm kind of spooked by that old guy, too."

Cole nodded as they walked. "What if the bowling ball hit him? He could really get hurt."

"Uh, *hurt*? It would kill him!" Peter exclaimed. "He would look like roadkill—like he'd been run over by a semi. It would crush his skull like a smashed watermelon. All his brains would—"

"Okay, okay, I get the picture," Cole said. "So do you

have to head home right away?"

"Not if I call my mom. Why?"

"Maybe we could just hang out."

Peter smiled. "Maybe we can try being invisible."

After Peter called his mother, they walked aimlessly for several blocks. Both were in their own worlds, lost in thought, when suddenly they heard footsteps and turned. Keith and his friends had crept up behind them. "Hey, bear bait!" Keith said, a cocky smirk on his face. "Are you two deaf?"

Cole wanted to kick himself for not paying attention.

"Time for the secret weapon," Peter whispered, sliding his hand inside the pocket of his baggy pants to activate the cell phone.

"What did you say, gimp?" asked Keith.

Peter spoke loudly, his words slow and deliberate. "I a-a-asked you what you're going to do to us now that y-y-you caught us two blocks away from school?"

"We're g-g-going to do what we should have d-d-done yesterday," Keith mocked.

"What have we done to you guys?" Cole asked. But he knew they didn't need a reason. He had never needed a reason himself when he used to beat kids up. He knew exactly how Keith and his friends thought, and it scared him.

"Maybe I don't like you," said Alex, a skinny blond kid from Cole's math class.

Cole glanced around. Peter's saying they were two blocks away from the school didn't help the principal much if she was listening. Cole pointed to a yellow house nearby. "You better leave us alone—the principal lives in that house," he said loudly. "Two forty-six Elm Street."

Peter looked quizzically at Cole and then grinned. "Oh, yeah, she l-l-lives at two forty-six Elm Street," he repeated slowly.

"What a crock of bull—," Keith said. "You think we're stupid?" He shoved Peter. "If the principal lives there, my mother lives in an igloo."

Peter was scared, but the cell phone gave him confidence and he smiled. "Where did your mom get an igloo?" he asked.

Keith slapped Peter hard. "Get that grin off your face, retard," he said, "or I'll wipe it off."

Cole saw the group smirking and knew they were the most dangerous when they were showing off to one another. Quickly he sat down on the sidewalk and pulled Peter down beside him. "Don't say anything more," he whispered. "Be invisible."

"What are you doing now?" Keith asked.

"We're not going to fight you," Cole said. "If it makes you feel big and strong to hurt somebody who's sitting down, go ahead."

"I don't care if you're sleeping," Keith said, kicking Cole in the ribs.

Raw fear showed in Peter's eyes as Keith turned and kicked him, too. Eddy stepped forward and kicked Peter in the back. Cole was desperate to stop Peter from getting hurt. "Hey, dog breath!" he shouted. "Why don't you kick somebody your own size?"

Eddy and Keith laughed as they both kicked Cole at the same time.

Lying on his side, grimacing, Cole could see cars passing on the street. Drivers turned to look, but none stopped to help. Another hard kick in the chest took Cole's breath away, then he heard Peter grunt from being kicked again. Cole looked up at Keith. "Five against two isn't exactly fighting like a man."

"Okay, then get up and fight just me," Keith said.

"Yeah, right," Cole said. "And if I whup you, your friends are going to just sit back and watch. I don't think so. I'm not *that* stupid."

"You sure talk a lot for somebody who is getting his butt kicked." Keith kicked Cole again.

Suddenly a blue station wagon swerved to a stop beside the curb, and Ms. Kennedy stepped out.

The group started to run.

"Stop, or I call the police," the principal shouted. "I recognize every one of you. Line up, now!"

Reluctantly, the gang returned and shuffled into position. Cole and Peter stood, clutching their bruised ribs. Peter's nose was bleeding, and Ms. Kennedy handed him a tissue. "Are you okay?" she asked.

Peter nodded.

"What are you doing here?" Keith asked the principal timidly.

"I want to know what *you're* doing here," she replied.

"We didn't do nothing to them!" exclaimed Eddy.

"Oh, let me guess," the principal said. "Peter and Cole just walked up to you again, and this time they sat down on the sidewalk in front of you so they could relax and enjoy your company."

"We weren't really hurting them," Alex said.

"We were just messing with their heads a little," said Keith.

"Yeah, we were just joking," the others agreed.

"Maybe we should joke with you a little," Peter said.

Ms. Kennedy's voice grew cold. "You five are the biggest cowards in our school. Instead of these two, why don't you pick on the football team?"

The group remained silent, smirking.

Ms. Kennedy moved slowly, looking into the boys' eyes until each looked away, then she shouted, "You do *not* have the right to destroy someone else's dignity because you have none yourself!"

Cole was surprised by how the principal was acting. It took a lot of guts, but he still doubted anything would come of it. There weren't consequences in this school, not like on the island. There, if he chopped wood and covered it, he had dry wood for the winter. If not, he didn't. If he attacked a bear, it mauled him. If he gave it space, it trusted him. He wished Keith had to face consequences for his actions, but he knew that wasn't how it was at this school.

"Cole, you and Peter go on home, but stop by my office in the morning," Ms. Kennedy said. "I'll meet the rest of you back in my office in five minutes. Anybody that gets there after me pays the fiddler double."

Keith started toward the school, sauntering casually to prove he wasn't intimidated.

CHAPTER 5

A S COLE AND Peter headed down the sidewalk, Cole elbowed his friend. "Hey, your secret weapon worked."

"Yeah," Peter said with a grin. Then he grimaced.

"Are you okay?"

Peter wiped blood from his face. "The principal can't stop Keith and his friends."

"Seeing Keith slap you this afternoon made me want to pound his head against a sidewalk," Cole said. "I want to see *him* stutter and stammer the rest of his life. Maybe I should just beat him up and let the Circle send me to jail."

Tears filled Peter's eyes. "You going to jail won't make anything better. You're my only real friend."

"Sitting in a dumb freezer and carrying bowling balls isn't helping."

"I agree," Peter said, "but please don't go to jail."

★ ★ ★

Cole didn't tell his mother about Keith and the bullies or having to go see the principal, just that they weren't going to sit in the freezer anymore. He felt like he needed to work things out for himself. Weary, he went to bed early.

All that night, he tossed and turned, his dreams confused, his body aching. One moment the Spirit Bear was mauling him, and the next instant his dad was whipping him with the buckle end of the belt. Then the Circle was sending him back to jail. Finally, in his last dream, his totem pole had become a monster, threatening to attack him. When Cole's alarm went off, he felt like a zombie. He hugged his bruised ribs and grimaced as he crawled from his bed to get ready for school.

"Are you sure you don't want a ride?" his mother asked as they ate breakfast.

"I'm sure."

"Are you okay?" she asked. "You're awfully quiet this morning."

"I'm fine—I just need time alone."

Cole finished eating and gave his mother a quick kiss on the cheek. "Love you, Mom," he said. "Remember, tonight's the Circle."

"I love you, too," she said warmly, nodding.

As he walked to school, Cole's thoughts were as troubled as his dreams. Yesterday, a cell phone had saved their hides, but what if there had been no cell phone? Then what? And tonight, would the Circle members still think of him as a punk troublemaker? It bothered him that his dad wasn't coming. He was tempted to just show up at his office downtown to see what he'd do.

When Cole got to school, he went straight to the main office to wait. Peter arrived a few minutes later, and together they went in to see Ms. Kennedy.

"That was a slick trick you pulled yesterday," she said. "Where did you get my number?"

"It was on one of the teacher's desks," Peter admitted.

"I don't want students in the school running around with my cell phone number."

"I d-d-didn't give it to anybody," Peter said, lowering his head. His voice showed disappointment. "It seemed like a good idea."

"So what happened to the guys that picked on us?" Cole asked.

"I gave them detention for a week."

"Detention won't change anything," Cole said. "It won't stop the bullying. What are we supposed to do the next time they get in our face? Now they're even more ticked at us."

"If they bother either of you, report it to me or one of your teachers."

"After we've been beat up," Cole said. "Detention won't change that."

"Those five will get suspended if this happens again."

"I doubt that," Cole said. "They know there aren't real consequences, otherwise they wouldn't be bullies." Cole bit back his anger. "Every day kids are getting hassled and nobody sees it or does anything about it."

"Each person has to do his part," Ms. Kennedy said. "It

was good that you didn't fight back yesterday."

"You don't get it, do you?" Cole said angrily. "This isn't about us not fighting back. When I was a bully, the more somebody refused to fight, the more I picked on him. Don't you see, I'm screwed no matter what I do? If I use my fists, I go to jail. If we do nothing, we get used as punching bags."

"Use your brains," Ms. Kennedy said curtly.

"We d-d-did that," Peter exclaimed. "We used the cell phone, and you didn't like that."

Ms. Kennedy reached across her desk and gathered papers into her hands. "There's no easy answer. You two need to get to class now."

After school, Cole found Peter near the bulldog statue. With school back in session, fresh gang symbols appeared each morning on the crumbling pedestal.

"What do you want to do if we're not going to drop bowling balls?" Peter asked.

"Maybe we can look for a place to be invisible."

"All right," Peter said. "Let's go someplace really quiet."

Ten minutes later, they were still looking for a spot when they heard wild swearing and shouting. Ahead, they spotted two boys hassling the old homeless man from the abandoned building. One boy had tipped over his cart as the other taunted him.

At first the grizzled man brandished his whittling knife each time one of the tormentors ventured near, but soon he knelt and cowered, pulling the dirty white blanket tightly around his shoulders. Cole remembered cowering the same way when his father had whipped him with a belt. As Peter and Cole watched, one of the boys grabbed the man's blanket. The bum clung to it desperately, but the boy yanked it away, laughing.

"Knock it off!" Cole shouted, breaking into a run.

At that moment, a police car rolled into view, lights flashing. The two boys took off running. The homeless man picked up his blanket and retreated to his tipped-over cart, glaring wildly and brandishing his knife at the world.

The two police officers climbed from their car and drew their pistols as they approached the crazed man. Slowly they circled him, talking patiently and holding out their hands for the knife. Finally one officer grabbed the old tramp from behind and wrestled the knife from his hand. They handcuffed him.

Cole ran up. "Officer, it wasn't that guy's fault."

"And who are you?"

"I'm Cole Matthews. Two boys were hassling the old guy. They tipped over his cart and grabbed his blanket. He was just protecting himself."

The bum eyed Cole with quiet blue eyes.

"Do you know the boys who did it?" the officer asked.

Cole shook his head. "I didn't recognize them."

"No matter what, this guy can't be waving a knife at people," said the second officer.

Peter joined Cole beside the police car. "He just carves with it," Peter said. "We saw him whittling."

"We still have to take him in."

The patrol car drove off with the bum in handcuffs. His belongings were scattered on the ground: worn pieces of clothing, an old bowling trophy, a hand mirror, some broken toys, a bundle of clothes hangers, and ordinary trash as if the old guy was cleaning up the streets.

"Let's put it all back in the cart and push it over to the building where he lives," Cole said. "We'll leave it inside."

Quickly they picked up the scattered junk. They were almost finished when Peter called, "Hey, look at this!"

"What you got?" Cole asked.

Peter walked over and handed an object to Cole. "That's what the guy was carving."

Cole turned the small chunk of carved wood over in his hand. The guy had started carving a bear's head. It was amazingly lifelike.

Peter took the carving back from Cole. "Man, this thing looks real—I want to try and carve one just like it."

That night, Garvey brought his old station wagon by to pick up Cole and his mother for the Circle meeting. They all sat in the front seat. "So what have you and Peter been up to?" Garvey asked.

"Trying to pretend we're on the island again. For a pond, we sat in a freezer down at Frazier's grocery store. For ancestor rocks, we dropped bowling balls from an old abandoned building. But it's not working."

"You don't need ponds or ancestor rocks anymore," Garvey said. "Look at a leaf, glance up at the stars, or just close your eyes and breathe deeply. Go inside yourself to the place you're already at. The island taught you where that place was. Now all you have to do is *be* there."

"You make it sound so easy."

"Because it is. Don't fight it."

"I'll try," Cole promised.

"How about the Spirit Bear?" Garvey asked. "Have you seen the Spirit Bear?"

Cole looked over at Garvey quizzically. "We thought we did on Monday, but it was just an old man." Cole told Garvey and his mom about the homeless man being arrested. "When we picked up his stuff this afternoon, Peter found a bear head the old guy had started carving."

"That's a good sign," Garvey said.

"Yeah—isn't that a coincidence!"

"There are no coincidences," Garvey said. "Remember that." His face turned serious. "I don't like that you two dropped bowling balls from an abandoned building."

"We already quit doing that. It was a mistake."

"A stupid mistake."

"Hey, didn't you ever make mistakes at my age?"

Garvey nodded. "Plenty of mistakes—but I also discovered that if you're where you should be in your heart and spirit, you don't make those mistakes. Cole, your heart and spirit not being in the right place really scares me."

When Cole arrived at the Circle, half the chairs were already filled. He recognized the Keeper, the plump woman who had led the Circle that banished him to the island. Others from that meeting sat chatting quietly. One new face surprised him. "Ms. Kennedy, what are you doing here?" he whispered.

"Garvey invited me. Do you mind?"

"Uh, no," Cole said nervously. Sitting down, he glanced around the room for any other surprises. Peter arrived, but his parents made him sit on the opposite side of the Circle.

At exactly seven o'clock, the Keeper stood and walked to the center of the group. As she called the meeting to order, everyone stood and joined hands as they had in previous Circles. This time, Cole found himself holding hands with his mother and Garvey. The last time, he had been between both his parents. Now his father was absent.

The Keeper began with a simple prayer—but it wasn't a prayer to God, like in a church. It was a prayer to the powers that surrounded and filled all things. It was a prayer of honor and thankfulness.

Then the Keeper held up a large brown hawk feather. "This feather symbolizes honesty and respect. No one may speak without holding this feather. When you speak, speak from your heart. Tonight I'm beginning our Circle by letting Peter and Cole each tell of their experiences on the island. And then I would like Cole's parole officer to tell of his experiences with the boys and how he thinks Cole has changed." The Keeper turned to Ms. Kennedy. "I've also invited their new principal, Ms. Kennedy, to share her experiences with Peter and Cole since their return. Then we'll pass the feather around the full Circle."

As the Keeper handed him the feather, Cole tried to remain calm. It felt like he was telling someone else's story when he described trying to escape from the island, being mauled by the Spirit Bear, and the night he began to change—a stormy night spent worrying about sparrows in a tree. "Lightning struck the tree," Cole explained. "The sparrows were so helpless and innocent—they didn't deserve to die. I couldn't save them, but it was the first time that I cared about something other than myself."

Cole finished by telling about Peter coming to the island and how they had become friends. "Before I left the island, Peter helped me carve a Circle on my totem. I wanted a Circle because Garvey taught me that our lives are a part of something bigger that touches all things. Every part of a Circle is both a beginning and an end, and in a Circle, everything is one."

The Keeper smiled as Cole handed back the speaking feather. She handed it next to Peter.

"I don't talk as good as Cole 'cause he kind of d-d-did a job on me," Peter stammered. "But he had pretty bad stuff happen to him, too, when he was young. On the island, I figured out that he w-w-wasn't the monster I thought." Peter grinned. "He can still be a jerk when I beat him at cards."

The group laughed, but Peter continued seriously. "Cole has changed. One day on the island I got mad at him and he let me beat him up really bad without fighting back. I know I shouldn't have done that, but I was still really mad."

Peter toyed with the feather, then looked directly at Cole. "I didn't think I would ever say this, but now Cole is my best friend."

When Garvey was handed the feather, he said, "I went through banishment myself as a child—that is why I wanted Cole to have the experience. Nothing on the island went the way we planned, but I have watched two boys grow and change in front of my eyes." Garvey considered his next words. "Their battles aren't over yet," he said, "but I think they've both proved they're mature enough to fight those battles. Any punishment for Cole at this time would be counterproductive."

Cole waited nervously for Ms. Kennedy to speak. One word from her about the fight with Keith could send him to jail.

Ms. Kennedy turned the feather in her hand slowly. "I didn't know either Cole or Peter before this school year," she began. "It hasn't been easy for them coming back to the city. I do know what they're going through, and if they're willing to try, I think they'll make it."

Instead of relief, Cole felt a flash of anger. He and Peter were already trying as hard as they could and it wasn't working! Ms. Kennedy didn't have a clue what they were going through!

When the Keeper started the feather around the full Circle, everyone, including Peter's parents, agreed that Cole had changed during his banishment to the island. The group's recommendation to the court was to place Cole on continued probation for the next two years. If Cole stayed out of trouble during that time, his record would be cleared. If not, jail would be the automatic next step.

The Keeper asked, "Does anybody else wish to speak?"

Cole held his hand forward for the feather. "Garvey said that Peter and I were mature enough now to fight our own battles here at home, but he's wrong," Cole began. "Since we got back, kids have been all over us, picking on us and wanting to fight. They get to me by picking on Peter. I won't let them hurt Peter, but if I fight them, I go to jail. If I don't fight them, they'll hurt him. They call me psycho, and they call Peter gimp and retard." Cole's voice grew desperate and he swallowed the anger that was growing in his throat. "I don't know what to do. I'm scared. We'll do whatever you tell us to do."

The feather went around the Circle again.

Ms. Kennedy wasn't much help. "There are so many problems," she said. "Why should educators discipline a student and risk ending up in a lawsuit? What motivation is there for a tenured teacher to try harder? Many have given up and don't care anymore."

An awkward silence filled the room as the feather continued around the Circle and other solutions and ideas for the bully problem were discussed. When the feather arrived back at the Keeper, she asked one last time, "Does anybody have anything else they would like to add?"

Again Cole raised his hand. Holding the feather, he looked around the Circle. "I have two last things to say. First, thanks for not giving up on me—I really mean that." He paused, then looked directly at Ms. Kennedy and pinched the feather tightly. "Excuses don't help me. Tomorrow, or the next day, when the bullies catch me away from the school, I still don't know what to do."

★ ★ ★

Garvey was quiet as he drove Cole and his mother home. When he stopped in their driveway, he turned and said, "Cole, I'm proud of your honesty in the Circle tonight. And I'm even more proud of you for being able to admit your fear. That takes a big person."

Cole shrugged. "I still don't know what to do," he said. "When it comes right down to a bully in my face, what should I do?"

"I told you before, fight 'em!" Garvey said. "Just don't use your fists."

"I already tried sitting down and not fighting back— that didn't work," Cole said. "And we tried using the cell phone—Ms. Kennedy didn't like that."

Garvey shook his head. "There are other ways to fight."

"Like what?" Cole asked, as he and his mother got out of the car.

"You'll figure it out," Garvey said. He waved good-bye and backed out of the driveway.

"That man can be such a jerk," Cole said.

CHAPTER 6

COLE WELCOMED THE last bell on Friday, the end of his first week back in school. On the island, time had passed with the changing of light and weather. Now it changed with a clock, a calendar, and bells that marked the painfully slow passing of each school day.

Peter met Cole on the front steps. "I've decided to find the homeless guy and give him back his carving," he announced. "Want to go along?"

Cole hesitated.

"You're scared of him, aren't you?"

"After seeing him swinging his knife at the police, I'm not excited about going anywhere near him."

Peter held up the unfinished bear head. "I wanted to keep this, but it's not mine." He held out a second carved head, the same size but not as lifelike. "I carved this to give him."

"Why?"

Peter shrugged. "To show him we're okay. W-w-we

scare him as much as he scares us."

"I'll help you look, but what if he's dangerous?"

"And what if you're still dangerous?" Peter asked.

After wandering the streets for almost an hour, Cole suggested, "Maybe we can go to the abandoned building and leave the carving in his cart."

"Okay, but let's stop by my house and get flashlights. I want to check out the basement," Peter said.

"You want to get us killed?"

Peter grinned.

Half an hour later, Cole and Peter slipped quietly past the broken doors into the abandoned building. They found the cart of junk had disappeared from under the stairwell. Quietly they tiptoed to the head of the stairs that led down into the darkened basement.

"Hello!" Peter called out hesitantly.

"Anybody down there?" Cole hollered.

Hearing no sound, they snapped on their flashlights and started down the steps. A moldy odor filled the air.

"It's probably rotting bodies," Peter whispered.

Cole gave Peter a poke. "Knock it off—you're giving me the creeps." He shined his light slowly in a circle. The large room was nearly thirty feet across with cobwebs hanging from the ceiling. An old mattress had been placed in one corner. It was covered neatly with a ragged blanket. A big cardboard box served as a table.

Suddenly footsteps sounded on the floor overhead. Both boys snapped off their flashlights and held their breaths.

The footsteps stopped.

"Let's get out of here," Cole whispered, bounding up the stairs. Peter followed on his heels. Emerging at the top of the steps, they stopped cold in their tracks. Barely twenty feet away, the old homeless man stood, crouched as if he were warding off an attack. A deep growl sounded in his throat.

"We're just here to bring this b-b-back," Peter stammered, holding out the bear carving. He bent down and placed the carving on the floor. "W-w-we found it the day the police arrested you." His voice shook as he laid his own carving beside the first. "That's f-f-for you, too."

Not waiting for a reply, Cole and Peter backed between the broken front doors, then turned and ran, bumping into each other as they escaped. Not until they were well away from the building did they stop to look back. The old man was standing in the doorway watching them with curious eyes.

"That's how the Spirit Bear used to watch us," Peter said. Then he turned and kept running.

Saturday morning, Cole helped his mother carry in potted plants she'd bought at the nursery. Then he headed to the mall to see if Peter was around. It didn't matter what Peter's parents agreed to in the Circle, they still didn't want Peter near him.

Cole decided to enjoy the warm fall day while he waited for Peter. He sat on the grass near the main entrance, listening to the hectic sounds of the city: horns, car engines, sirens, and kids shouting. While he waited, he closed his eyes and relaxed.

A breeze carried mist from a nearby sprinkler onto his face, and Cole imagined a waterfall crashing over rocks into a deep, cold pool. Other sounds gradually melted together and softened. Cole breathed in deeply, enjoying the pungent smell of fresh-cut grass.

He and Peter had become invisible on the island when they learned to be quiet and blend in with all that surrounded them. The wind, the rain, all living things were part of something bigger, part of the Circle. Sitting on the grass, Cole felt important for being a part of something that was so big and so wonderful. At the same time he felt insignificant, smaller than a speck of dust in the universe.

Cole heard a mother drag a screaming child from the mall and imagined a screaming osprey diving on a fish. The honking of a horn became the hooting of an owl on a dark night. Every sound and sensation around Cole became something natural, gradually melting into something bigger. Before long he was in another world, floating farther and farther away, out into space among the stars with no limitations, no boundaries, and no problems. With each breath, his body dissolved more, finally becoming a part of everything around him. Invisible.

It seemed only minutes before Cole opened his eyes, but a clock above the mall entrance showed that over an hour had passed. A squirrel sat motionless barely two feet away, holding a nut between its front paws and staring at him. Cole sensed another presence. Slowly he looked around. Gone were the waterfalls and osprey. Once again the sounds of honking horns, screaming children, and busy shoppers bombarded the air. Cars maneuvered around one another in the busy parking lot.

And then Cole spotted him.

The homeless man stood across the parking lot near the gas station, his hands resting on his shopping cart of junk. He stared at Cole with calm, penetrating eyes. Cole stared back for a moment and then lowered his gaze. When he glanced up seconds later, the man had disappeared— simply vanished. For several long minutes, Cole searched but saw nothing. Finally he lay back on the grass.

The old man puzzled him, but other things began making sense. Garvey had said that the pond, the ancestor rocks, and the dances were all simple tools. He said that being a part of the Circle was easy because it meant going to a place you were already at.

And that was what had happened today. Today there had been no ritual, no tricks, no tools. Just quietness. That was all Cole had needed. Feeling calm inside for the first time in days, he stood and started for home. He couldn't wait to tell Peter about this afternoon.

He had only walked a block from the mall when he spotted Keith and his gang coming down the street toward him. Keith walked boldly in front of the rest, a wicked grin on his lips.

At first Cole thought to turn and run, but running would simply delay the inevitable. In a way, not having Peter around made this a good time for a showdown. But how would he fight Keith? He hugged his injured arm close to his bruised ribs and kept walking.

Keith angled across the street, looking unsure because Cole wasn't avoiding him. "Hey, psycho," he shouted. "You're going to get your butt kicked!"

Cole still didn't know what he was going to do. His mind scrambled as the bullies approached. Garvey had said there were ways to fight without fists.

"You're history, bush boy," Keith said. "Where's your retard friend?"

Cole breathed deeply and for a moment quit trying to think. Instead, he just stared at the boys with a strange sense of calm. And that was when it came to him. He spoke deliberately to Keith. "Before you touch me, you have three choices."

"And what's that, bear bait?" mocked Keith. "To kick your butt left, right, or straight ahead?"

The group laughed loudly.

"So what are my choices?" Keith asked sarcastically.

"I'm not going to fight you, so you can either leave me alone—"

"No chance of that," taunted Keith. "Try again."

Cole continued calmly, "Or beat me up."

"That's a good plan," Keith said. "I like that one."

Cole nodded. "Of course, if you choose that one, I will file charges."

"You squeal on us, we'll kill you!" Keith said. "What's my third choice?"

"You just said it—kill me." Cole met Keith's stare with

his own. "Those are your only choices today. Either leave me alone, beat me up and I file charges, or . . ." Cole paused for effect. "Or kill me."

Keith's laugh sounded weaker.

"I'm serious," Cole said. "So what's it going to be? I'm not afraid of you."

"You think we're afraid of you reporting us?" Keith said.

"Yes, you're scared stiff. And if you do kill me, one of you will rat out the rest and you will all spend the rest of your lives behind bars. It won't be with other cheap punks. It'll be with real killers and rapists. So what are you going to do?"

"You sure talk tough," said Keith, punching Cole hard in the gut. "I'm tired of your talk, motor mouth."

"Now I'm filing charges against you," Cole gasped, and then turned to the others. "Who else wants charges filed?"

"Oh, we're really afraid of you," Keith taunted, giving Cole a hard shove that sent him stumbling backward. Keith looked back at his friends. "What's wrong? You guys afraid of this loser?"

"You've already dug your grave," Cole told Keith. "Maybe your friends aren't as stupid."

"You're pissing me off," Keith shot back. "We're not afraid of you!" He swung hard at Cole and knocked him to the ground.

Cole sat up slowly, rubbing blood from his nose and mouth. "You *should* be afraid," he said calmly.

Keith looked back at his friends. "Are you losers going

to just stand there staring?" he shouted.

"I'm not getting in trouble with the police," Eddy said. "My dad will kill me."

"Me, either," announced Alex.

Keith's four friends backed slowly away from Cole. "Just leave him be," one said. "He's crazy."

Keith gave Cole an angry kick in the chest. "Chicken turds!"

Cole spit blood on the sidewalk and rubbed his ribs. "You might as well kill me now," he said. "I'm going straight to the police department. This is assault."

Keith looked uncertain, glancing up the street as if watching for the police. "Hey, look, can't you take a joke?" he said suddenly.

Cole stood and pointed at the sidewalk. "If this blood is a joke, I'm not laughing. Unless you plan to kill me, I'm headed to the police station." Cole turned and started walking.

"You squealer! You rat!" Keith shouted after him. "I'll tell everyone at school you ratted on me!"

Cole kept walking.

Cole's mother gasped, holding her hand over her mouth when he entered the house with a bloody face and torn clothes. "What happened?" she cried.

Cole told how he'd been beaten up by Keith. "I'm filing charges," he announced. "Will you go with me?"

"Okay," she said, grabbing a wet washcloth. "But let's wipe that blood off your face first."

Cole pushed her hand away. "I want the police to see what Keith did."

When they arrived at the police station, Cole's mother helped to file the report and press charges. The officer on duty took pictures of Cole's face and chest.

Afterward, Cole wanted to stop by Garvey's.

"Can't that wait?" his mother asked.

"No, I want him to see what happened, too. He'll be proud I didn't fight back with my fists."

Fifteen minutes later they pulled into the drive of Garvey's small home near the Interstate. Garvey was working in the yard but threw down his rake when Cole climbed from the car holding his ribs, blood still smeared on his cheeks. "What the devil happened to you?" Garvey exclaimed, running over.

As Cole explained, Garvey examined his face and bruised ribs. "Did Keith do all this to you?"

Cole nodded. "I told him he'd better kill me 'cause I was pressing charges. And I did. We just came from the police station—that'll teach him to mess with me."

Garvey let out a slow breath. "He'll leave you alone now only because he's afraid of you."

"Good," Cole said, "'cause I had no other choice."

"You always have other choices," Garvey said.

"How would you have kept from getting beat up?" Cole shot back, frustrated. "And don't say, 'I'll figure it out.'"

Garvey shrugged. "Some days are just bad days. When bullies corner you, you're having a bad day—not much you can do about changing that." He shook his head slowly. "What's important is if you behave in a way that preserves your dignity and helps make tomorrow better."

"I did that!" Cole snapped, feeling his smoldering anger grow.

Garvey closed his eyes and rubbed his forehead as if he had a headache. "Filing charges used the same tool the bullies used—fear."

Cole threw his hands in the air. "Nothing I do will ever satisfy you! I'm not supposed to fight with my fists. Ms. Kennedy didn't like us using the cell phone. Sitting down didn't help. Now I'm not supposed to use my head."

"Nobody has the right to do this to you. Nobody! Cole, it's okay that you filed charges. All I'm saying is that you have other choices. There are times you fight with your fists—that's called violence. There are times when you lie down—that's called pacifism. What you guys did with the cell phone worked, but that was trickery. And sometimes, like today, you fought with a threat—that's fear. But there are other choices."

"Like what?" Cole could feel his anger taking over. "You're just messing with my head."

Garvey reached out and tapped Cole's chest. "Try fighting with your heart sometime."

Cole pushed Garvey's hand away. "What? Send Keith flowers? Give him a kiss?"

Garvey winked. "You'll figure it out," he said.

"You talk big!" Cole shouted. He clenched his fists, wishing he could knock the smug look off Garvey's face.

"You don't have any more answers than me! Why don't *you* try and—"

Cole's mother grabbed his arm. "It's time for us to leave now," she said, tugging him forcefully toward the car.

Cole pulled away. "I'm okay," he said, trying to shake off his anger. Glancing back, he saw disappointment in Garvey's eyes.

CHAPTER 7

T HE FOLLOWING DAY, Sunday, Peter convinced his
mother to let him hang out with Cole.

"What happened?" Peter exclaimed when he saw
Cole's puffy lip and swollen eye. "A truck hit you?"

Cole explained all that had happened. "You should
have seen the look in their eyes when I told them they
would have to kill me," he said.

"What if they had killed you?" Peter asked.

"They'd have gone to jail."

"That wouldn't help you much."

"They would never really kill me."

"You don't know that," Peter argued.

"Now you're sounding like Garvey. Everybody criti-
cizes what I do, but nobody has a better idea."

"What did Garvey say to do?" Peter asked.

"He wants me to give Keith flowers and kiss him,"
Cole said sarcastically.

"Really? He said that?"

"Not exactly, but he said to fight with my heart."

"So take your heart and throw it at Keith," Peter said, grinning. "Maybe he'll get a concussion. The blood will splatter all over, and your heart will bounce around on the ground beating, and—"

"Okay! Okay!" Cole interrupted. "Hey, Peter, yesterday I sat in front of the mall and became invisible."

"Like on the island?"

Cole nodded. "And remember how we sometimes saw the Spirit Bear appear and disappear? Well yesterday, I opened my eyes and found that old homeless guy staring at me across the parking lot. I looked down for just a few seconds, and when I looked back he was gone."

"That's weird," Peter said. "I was thinking about that old guy, too. His carving looked so real and it wasn't even finished yet. I wonder where he learned to carve."

"There's lots of things about him I wonder about."

"So, where can we go today to be invisible?" Peter asked.

Cole glanced down the street thoughtfully. "Just for the fun of it, let's try someplace really noisy again—like in the park."

"Sounds good," Peter agreed, starting out excitedly.

Cole eyed his friend as they walked. Getting slapped and kicked by Keith could easily have taken Peter back into depression, but he was hanging in there.

Reaching the park, they picked a comfortable patch of grass under a big Norway pine. Nearby, teenagers laughed and shouted, throwing a Frisbee. Parents called to their children. A baby cried nonstop, and two barking dogs kept chasing each other.

"We'll go so far into the quiet of our minds that we won't even hear the sounds," Cole said.

"Okay," Peter said doubtfully, closing his eyes.

Cole did the same, breathing in deeply.

At first, random thoughts bombarded him, so he focused and imagined the Spirit Bear standing on the shoreline of the island. He imagined a drop of rain landing on its white fur and then slowly running down the side of the big animal until it finally dripped onto the ground.

Cole almost let the thought end there, but then he drew in another breath and followed the raindrop as it soaked into the soil, wetting the root of a tree. Slowly the tree absorbed the moisture, drawing it upward through the trunk until it reached the branches and leaves. Gently the wind absorbed the moisture and carried it to the sky to help form another cloud. Soon, another drop of rain fell from the sky, landing on the Spirit Bear.

Another Circle was complete.

Cole slowly opened his eyes and looked around the park, half expecting to see the homeless man again. All he found was noise and commotion, but he felt calm.

Peter's eyes were already open. "You were gone a long time," he said. "What were you thinking about?"

"About rain falling on the Spirit Bear," Cole answered. "How about you?"

Peter shrugged. "I couldn't think of anything 'cause

dogs were barking and the baby kept crying. I wanted the dogs to go over and bark at the baby."

The second week back, things grew worse. The school's crowded stairwells and dark narrow hallways were like a madhouse with kids slamming lockers, shouting, shoving, and tripping one another. As usual, most of the teasing and bullying was ignored by the teachers.

Keith and his bunch mimicked Cole's injured right arm by purposely hugging an arm in close to their waists as they passed him in the hallway. Alex pretended it was an accident when he bumped Cole hard with a shoulder and tripped him.

In study hall, Keith approached Cole's table. "Hey, you turd!" he growled under his breath. "You didn't have to press charges just because I shoved you a little. What a weenie."

Cole pulled up his shirt to show the large bruises on his rib cage. "You call this a little shove?"

"My parents are all bent out of shape," Keith said. "You drop those charges or I swear I'll—"

"Or you'll what?" Cole interrupted. "Kill me?"

Leaving, Keith gave Cole's chair a hard shove.

Cole knew he and Peter weren't the only ones bullied. Midweek, he noticed some football players teasing a student with Down syndrome by using baby talk to her face. He also spotted four girls following the thin girl he'd seen teased the first day of school. Fear haunted the girl's eyes as her tormentors mimicked her every move.

Something else kept weighing on Cole's mind. Finally

he had to do something about it. Thursday, when Peter met him after school, Cole excused himself. "I need to be alone," he said.

"Can't we be alone together?"

"I'm going to go see my dad."

"For real?"

Cole nodded.

"Does he know you're coming?"

Cole shook his head. "I'll tell you how things go."

Peter waved good-bye, and soon Cole was on the bus headed downtown to his father's office.

"Well, hello," the secretary said when Cole walked in. "Haven't seen you in a while. Let me check and see if your dad's free."

"If he's not with someone, I'd like to surprise him," Cole said.

Hesitating, she motioned Cole toward the closed door. "Okay, go on in."

Cole nearly chickened out. He knocked cautiously, then turned the handle and eased the door open far enough to poke his head inside. His father sat behind a large desk, wearing a suit and tie. At first he didn't look up from his work. When he did, surprise and hostility showed in his eyes. "What are you doing here?" he asked.

Cole entered and closed the door behind him. "I just came to see you."

His father rocked back in his chair. "So what do you want from me now?"

"Nothing, Dad, I just wanted to know how you're

doing. I haven't seen you since last year."

"How did you expect me to be doing? Your mother won custody of you with her abuse charges. Social Services is all over me, the divorce cost me a mint, and my business is half what it used to be."

"Is that all that's important to you?" Cole asked. "The money and your reputation?"

"What else is there? I gave up on *you* years ago."

Cole wasn't sure what to say next. Listening to his father, he felt like he was standing on a train track with a freight train barreling toward him. "Dad, this isn't about anybody's money or reputation. It's about you and me. It's about our family."

"In case you haven't noticed, we don't have a family anymore, thanks to you."

Cole's voice trembled. "I've been a real jerk, Dad, but I'm trying to make things right."

"It's too late for that—you and your mother already messed up my life."

"Mom filed charges because you drank and got violent. You started hitting me really hard."

"You deserved a good spanking."

"Getting drunk and hitting someone until he bleeds isn't a spanking," Cole said strongly.

"Keep your voice down," his father said, glancing toward the door. "So why are you really here?"

Cole swallowed the rush of feelings that threatened to flood his eyes with tears. "Dad, you never wrote me a single letter while I was gone."

"Wouldn't have done any good."

"You don't know that! Being on the island changed me," Cole said. "You have to believe that. We all make mistakes, but maybe things can be different now."

Cole's father stood, towering over Cole. His voice grew cold. "You get something through your dim-witted skull," he said. "I don't buy your act for one second. You haven't changed—you've never fooled me. I don't need you barging into my office causing any more problems. I'm busy now and have a lot to do, so unless you have something else to say, you need to leave." He motioned toward the door.

Cole started to go, and then turned back. "Dad, one more thing."

His father sat down heavily. "What now?"

"Mom quit drinking and is doing great."

"I'm so delighted," his father said with thick sarcasm, examining some papers he had picked up off his cluttered desk. "Anything else?"

"Yeah," Cole said, tears welling up in his eyes. "Dad, I miss you."

His father refused to look up.

Cole didn't want his father to see him cry so he rushed from the office and out onto the street. He blinked again and again in the bright sun. He had been such a fool to come down here. What had he expected—that his father would hug him and say he loved him and missed him?

Suddenly Cole felt empty inside. "Stupid! You're so stupid!" he mumbled to himself as he waited for the bus that would take him home.

CHAPTER 8

FRIDAY, COLE ARRIVED at school early and found the doors still locked. He hung out near the steps, apart from several other students who stood around the ratty bulldog statue, sneaking smokes.

The sound of a skateboard clattering down the sidewalk caused Cole to turn and look. He squinted into the bright morning sun. Skateboards weren't allowed on school grounds but nobody enforced the rule. The skater was only a dozen yards away when Cole realized it was Keith.

At that same instant, Keith spotted Cole. Kicking faster and laughing loudly, he changed direction, aiming straight at Cole. At the last second, Cole jumped aside. Keith swerved, too, but a wheel caught a crack in the sidewalk and sent him headfirst into the steps with a sickening grunt.

The students standing near the bulldog laughed as Keith writhed on the steps, holding his face. Blood gushed from his nose and mouth. Cole could see broken teeth and torn skin. Keith pulled himself down onto the sidewalk, then he collapsed and rolled onto his back, coughing and gagging on his own blood.

Cole hesitated, then rushed to Keith's side. He knelt down and pulled Keith's head over so he wouldn't choke. The students crowded around, but their laughter had stopped. "He's hurt—get help!" Cole shouted.

A couple of students ran toward the school.

"Someone call nine one one," Cole shouted.

A girl pulled out her cell phone and called as Cole held Keith firmly. Keith opened his eyes, glanced up, and their eyes met, then he closed his eyes again, grimacing in pain. Blood kept flowing from his mouth and nose.

"You'll be okay. You'll be okay," Cole repeated, as more students gathered to gawk. It reminded Cole of when he had been mauled by the Spirit Bear. He knew the feeling of being helpless. What if Keith was dying? It was weird, but for a moment Cole felt as if he were holding himself.

Finally several teachers came rushing across the lawn as the sound of a siren wailed toward the school. A red and white ambulance pulled into sight, lights flashing, and drove up on the sidewalk. Two paramedics jumped out and rushed to Keith's side. One took his pulse while the other checked his eyes and looked into his bloodied mouth.

"I've got his head now," said the paramedic, allowing Cole to stand and back away. They placed a big plastic collar around Keith's neck and strapped him to a backboard, then lifted him carefully into the waiting ambulance.

Covered with blood, Cole watched the ambulance pull away. The office secretary approached him. "Are you okay?"

Cole nodded.

"Thanks for helping," she said. "Go home and clean up. I'll have you excused from class until you get back."

When Cole arrived home, his mother still hadn't left for work. Coming from her bedroom, she spotted Cole, his T-shirt covered in blood. "Oh no!" she cried. "Did Keith do this to you again?"

"Keith wrecked his skateboard."

"Where are you hurt?"

"This is all his blood," Cole said. "I helped him. I held his head until the ambulance came."

"You helped him?"

"Someone had to."

All day, rumors of Keith's accident spread. After Cole returned to school, kids kept asking him what had happened.

"I guess he couldn't stop," Cole repeated.

"Did you make him fall?" one student asked.

"No," Cole replied firmly, haunted by the memory of Keith's scared eyes. He wondered if this accident would make Keith realize how foolish he was being.

When school finally ended, Cole stopped by the office to ask about Keith.

"He was admitted to the hospital," the secretary said.

"The one near the Interstate?"

She nodded, raising an eyebrow.

"Thanks."

Peter caught up to Cole as he headed out the front door. "Where are you going?" he asked.

Cole didn't feel much like explaining, but he didn't want to hurt Peter's feelings either. "I'm going to the hospital to check on Keith."

Peter wrinkled his forehead with a puzzled look. "Why are you doing that?" he asked. "He tried to run you over."

"I'm just going to see if he's okay."

"You're weird," Peter said. "I hope he hurt his brain! Can I go with you?"

Cole hesitated and then nodded. "Sure."

"Maybe we can go someplace afterward and try to be invisible again," Peter said.

Cole nodded but was lost in thought. The hospital was nearly a mile from school, and he doubted he would be allowed to see Keith when they got there. He still wasn't sure why he was going.

When they arrived, Cole asked for directions to Keith's room.

"Are you family?" the duty nurse asked.

Cole shook his head. "Just friends."

Peter frowned at Cole. "Friends?" he whispered. "Like mud."

The nurse motioned down the hall. "Room three fourteen. He's in bad shape, and his family is with him."

Cole hesitated outside Keith's room. He found himself

more afraid of facing Keith in a bed than on the street with his gang. Maybe he shouldn't have come. Taking a deep breath, he walked in.

Keith's parents were standing beside his bed. They turned and greeted Cole and Peter when they entered. "Thanks for stopping by," Keith's mother said.

Keith looked like a mummy with his face wrapped in gauze. Only his eyes showed. A straw protruded from his mouth through the gauze. Two holes allowed him to breathe through his nose. An IV bag hung beside the bed. A tube from it ran into Keith's arm—he was totally help-less, unable to talk or move. Fear flashed into his eyes when he saw Cole approach. His gaze darted around the room for help.

Cole fumbled with his words. "I just came to see how you're doing."

After staring up for a moment, Keith reached to his side and picked up a notepad and pen. Awkwardly he scribbled a message and handed it to Cole. The note said, *Why are you here?*

"To see how you're doing," Cole repeated. "I don't want you hurt."

Keith scribbled another note and handed it to Cole. It said, *Thanks for the help.*

"No big deal," Cole mumbled. "You were choking and bleeding—nobody else was helping you."

Keith stared up curiously.

Cole coughed and looked around. Keith's parents were

watching him. "Hey, we gotta run," Cole said to Keith. "I just wanted to check on you. Get better, okay."

"Yeah, g-g-get better," Peter said.

As Cole and Peter turned to leave, Keith's father stopped them. "Thanks for coming. I'm Troy Arnold, Keith's dad." He put out his hand. "And your names are?"

Cole shook his hand. "I'm Cole," he said. "And this is Peter."

The man frowned. "You're not Cole Matthews, the boy who filed assault charges against my son?"

"He beat me up pretty bad," Cole said, pointing to his own black eye and swollen cheek. He lifted his shirt to show his bruises.

Mrs. Arnold gasped. "Then why are you here today?"

Cole hesitated. "I'm not exactly sure, but I didn't want Keith hurt. I gotta get going."

"That was too weird," Peter said as they rode the elevator down to the main floor. "Way too weird. Why did you do that?"

Cole didn't answer.

"Hello, Planet Earth to Cole."

Cole stopped on the sidewalk outside the hospital and faced Peter. "When my mom gets home tonight, I'm going down to drop the charges against Keith."

Peter frowned. "You've really lost it now. First you visit Keith at the hospital and then you drop the charges? *Excuuuse* me! This is the jerk who beat you up and tried to run you over. You should be beating the snot out of him."

"I *am* still fighting him," Cole said, realizing it even as he spoke.

"By visiting him at the hospital and dropping charges?"

Cole nodded. "I'm fighting him with my heart."

Peter jabbed a finger in Cole's chest. "You're *really* weird."

Cole wanted to be quiet without hurting Peter's feelings, so he pointed to a small knoll just past the end of the parking lot. "Let's go sit on that hill and try to be invisible."

"Okay."

Soon both boys were sitting quietly on the grassy knoll, their eyes closed. This time Cole focused his mind simply on being empty. He pretended he was a big leaky bucket hanging from a hook, and every drip from the bucket made him emptier. The water dripped slower and slower and slower. For nearly an hour he imagined water leaking out until finally the bucket was completely dry and floated away into the sky. As the bucket disappeared, Cole opened his eyes.

He found two robins close by picking worms from the grass. Sensing another presence, Cole glanced up and caught his breath. Barely twenty feet away stood the old homeless man, his ragged white blanket draped over his shoulders. Baggy pants hung from his bony frame, but his shirt was tucked in and his pant cuffs were rolled up neatly so they didn't drag on the ground. The bum stood motionless on the grass, halfway between them and his cart. His gaze was relaxed, as if he had been standing there for some time.

Cole reached out and touched Peter's arm. Peter opened his eyes, blinked, and spotted the old man. He started to stand but stopped when the homeless man crouched and placed something in the grass. Without looking back, the man retreated and continued down the sidewalk, pushing his cart.

Peter jumped to his feet and ran to retrieve the object. "It's the same bear he was carving the day the police arrested him, except now it's finished," he exclaimed.

Cole took the miniature bear and rolled it in his fingers, tracing his thumb over the delicate body. "It looks real enough to start breathing," he said. "Why did he give it to us?"

"Maybe because I gave him the bear I carved," Peter said. "Or maybe he knows we returned his cart to him that day."

"Maybe," Cole said.

CHAPTER 9

T HAT EVENING, COLE told his mother he wanted to drop
charges against Keith.

"You're making a huge mistake," she argued.

"It's what I need to do," Cole insisted. He told her of
his visit to the hospital. "Do you remember when Garvey
said I should try fighting with my heart?"

"Are you sure this is what he meant?"

Cole wasn't sure of anything, but it seemed right. He
nodded.

"Okay then, let's go—I'll get the car keys," she said.

As Cole had figured, the police tried to talk him out of
dropping charges. "We need people to stand up and fight,"
the sergeant argued. "That's all thugs understand."

"I am fighting. In my own way."

"You're chickening out," the sergeant insisted.

Cole didn't know how to explain to the officer that it
had taken far more courage to visit Keith in the hospital

than to file charges or fight him with fists. A huge weight lifted off his shoulders as he walked from the police station. It was the first time in his life that he felt he had really won a fight, not by controlling Keith but by controlling his own reaction. This was what Garvey had been talking about.

Cole rode home with his mother, lost in thought. He had always assumed that when two people fought, someone needed to lose. But today, nobody had lost. Cole realized he had done more than make it hard for Keith to be an enemy. By preserving Keith's dignity, he had also saved his own.

It was a week before Keith returned to school, his cheeks and nose still bandaged. Cole spotted him in the hallway and approached him. "How are you doing?" he asked.

Distrust showed in Keith's eyes. "How does it look like I'm doing?"

"Man, you really crashed hard," Cole said. "Are you okay?"

"It hurts to talk and I have trouble breathing. Does that make you happy?"

"I didn't want you hurt," Cole said.

He could see Keith struggling with his emotions. "Thanks for dropping the charges," Keith said. "Why did you do that? And why did you help me when I crashed and then come to see me in the hospital?"

Cole shrugged. "To show you I wasn't a jerk."

Keith stared down at his shoes. "I'm the one who's been a jerk."

The bell rang.

"We better get going," Cole said, feeling the world lift from his shoulders.

Cole felt good to be sorting some things out for himself, but Minneapolis Central High still simmered with fear and anger. Tensions ran high, and each morning the bulldog's pedestal was tagged with new gang symbols. Many students feared coming to school. Cole wondered how long it would be before something boiled over.

His answer came all too soon.

That weekend the school was vandalized; windows were broken and paint was sprayed on the front doors.

After school on Monday, Cole was waiting patiently for Peter near the front entrance. Students milled around, talking and waiting for rides. When Peter didn't show, Cole returned inside. From the hallway, he spotted a commotion in the main office. Peter's parents were there, along with Ms. Kennedy and the school nurse, all crowding around someone in a chair. Cole ran in to find Peter, sitting bent over, clothes torn and face bruised and swollen. "What happened?" he cried.

Peter's father turned and gave Cole a shove. "Get away from our son."

Cole backed away and watched as Peter was helped to his feet and led, limping, from the office. His lip was cut and his eye was swollen, nearly closed.

"What happened?" Cole asked the secretary.

"He was attacked in one of the bathrooms. Somebody turned out the lights and beat him up."

Cole thought he might vomit. Peter had worked so hard and come so far—he didn't deserve this. Cole felt responsible. Stomach churning, he walked from the school and wandered aimlessly. He wished he was on a spaceship leaving Earth, never to return.

When he finally got home, Cole skipped eating and told his mother he didn't feel good. He spent the evening lying on his bed, staring at the ceiling.

The next morning at school, word of Peter getting beat up was overshadowed by news that one of the students had committed suicide by taking a bunch of drugs. It turned out to be the girl who'd been called a slut the first day of school—the one Cole had helped when she was hassled in the cafeteria. Her mother had found a note beside her bed saying she couldn't take being picked on anymore.

Talk of the suicide spread like wildfire. Cole walked the halls feeling numb. First the vandalism, then Peter's beating, and now this! His eyes filled with tears. It was crazy, so crazy. Suicide hadn't killed the girl. The kids who tormented her were the real killers.

After school, Cole returned home and called Peter's house. When there was no answer, he tried calling Garvey. As the phone rang and rang, Cole squeezed the handset harder. "C'mon! Don't they give parole officers answering machines?" he muttered with building frustration. He was about to hang up when Garvey answered.

"Hello?"

"Garvey, this is Cole. Did you hear about Peter getting beat up?"

"No, what happened?"

Cole tried to keep his voice from shaking. "Someone turned the lights out in the bathroom and beat him up really bad."

"How is he now?"

"I don't know. Nobody answers the phone. His parents won't let me near him. And then, last night, a girl at school committed suicide. This place is going crazy."

"Those are bad things," Garvey said plainly. "What are you doing about it?"

"The principal is the only one who can do anything, and she doesn't care," Cole said.

"There's always something you can do."

"It's not that easy," Cole protested. "I can't just snap my fingers and fix a whole school."

"Did I say it would be easy?" said Garvey. "But when the ground is torn up, that's when you plant seeds."

"We're not talking about farming here," Cole said. He fought to keep his voice calm. "This is something wrong with our whole stupid school."

"Then get busy," Garvey said.

"Doing what?"

"That's something you need to figure out for yourself."

"You're a big help," Cole snapped, slamming down the phone.

Frustrated, he walked back to the school grounds. Most of the students had left, but a few remained near a memorial that had been set up on the front lawn for the dead girl, Trish Edwards. Cole walked around the football field and gathered a handful of wildflowers. He placed them beside her picture with a note that said simply, *Nobody can pick on you now.* He signed his name, tears welling in his eyes.

The principal was heading to her car. She noticed Cole and walked over to him. "I'm sorry for what has happened to Peter and to Trish. Did you know her?"

Cole nodded. "A little. I knew something like this would happen if you didn't do something!"

Ms. Kennedy pressed a fist against her lips and blinked back tears. "I can't bring Trish back but I *am* doing something." Her voice shook as she continued. "I was so worried about my job, about pleasing parents, teachers, the superintendent, and school board members. All along, I should have been most concerned about the students."

"What *are* you doing?"

"You'll see tomorrow."

Cole watched the principal walk away. She looked tired, but she walked in a determined way that Cole had not noticed before.

The next morning, an assembly was called for the first period. Cole knew something was up—metal detectors, manned by police officers, had been installed inside both entrances.

On his way to the gym, Cole spotted Peter, who kept glancing around fearfully as he walked. His face was still swollen and bruised. Cole ran up to him. "Are you okay?"

he asked, surprised to see Peter back in school.

"No," Peter said without looking up. "I want to go back to the island where nobody can ever pick on me again."

"I want that myself," Cole said. They entered the gym to find half a dozen police officers patrolling the bleachers. Teachers who usually ignored all the shouting, shoving, and hitting were warning students who acted up.

"What is this? A drug bust?" one student shouted.

Ms. Kennedy stepped up to the microphone. At first she made no effort to quiet the students. She just stood and watched the chaos. Finally she tapped on the microphone and called out, "Okay, listen up everyone!"

"Shut up, you old witch!" a boy behind Cole shouted.

There was scattered laughter.

A teacher motioned for the student to come down from the bleachers.

"Go screw yourself!" the boy shouted, loudly enough to be heard across the gym.

Immediately a police officer came over, reaching for his handcuffs. "Come down now or you'll be arrested!" he shouted.

Surprised, the boy came down. He flashed a peace sign and grinned as he was led from the gym to prove he wasn't afraid. Cole guessed he was probably wetting his pants.

"Okay," Ms. Kennedy said, "who else would like to leave at this time?"

An uneasy hush fell over the gym. The principal continued. "This week, we had a suicide, an assault on a student, and major vandalism." Ms. Kennedy stopped and pointed at a girl who was grabbing another student's hair. An officer stepped in and led the girl away.

"What you just witnessed was assault," said the principal. "And that girl will be charged. If you shoved, kicked, or slapped a stranger downtown, you would be guilty of assault. The law does not change just because you are in a school.

"I don't want to hear anyone say 'I only teased some-one a little bit.' If you stab somebody a little or a lot, either way, you've stabbed him." She let the words sink in and then continued. "The biggest lie ever told to you is that sticks and stones may break your bones but words will never harm you. This week, words killed one of your class-mates.

"Words can be weapons, and beginning today, no stu-dent will speak to or touch any other student in a way that demeans, threatens, hurts, or causes even the slightest fear or intimidation. If you do, you're guilty of assault. As of today, this school has zero tolerance. And zero *means* zero!"

"Hey, Hitler, what happened to free speech?" yelled a student from the middle of the bleachers.

As he was led away, the principal held up her hand. "Let's talk about free speech. The Constitution of America, contrary to your belief, does not permit hate speech. Free speech is the freedom of *responsible* speech."

Cole looked across the bleachers. Most kids were lis-tening, but a few continued to yawn, talk, or harass others.

The principal studied the students. "You are probably wondering about the police officers. They are here to remind each of you that no one is above the law. Each day, if your behavior improves, there will be fewer officers. My hope is that your maturity and responsibility will allow them to leave soon.

"Also, as of now, this school has a dress code—the guidelines are now posted in the halls. Using gestures, colors, or symbols to intimidate others will no longer be allowed. Tomorrow, no student will be permitted in the school if he or she is not following those rules.

"Students, an education is money in your pockets. You let somebody rob you of that, you are letting them steal money from you. Now, unless there are questions, the gym will be dismissed one section at a time beginning on the east side. There will be no standing until your section is called. Anyone who shouts will be detained."

The principal removed her glasses in thought, and then stepped back to the microphone. "Students," she said, "hiring more police officers or passing more rules isn't a solution for what happened here. I challenge each of you to ask yourself what you personally might have done to contribute to this week's senseless tragedies. How could you have helped prevent them? Each of us carries blame, including me. Nothing will ever change unless *we* change."

All of this was too little, too late, Cole thought as he left the gym. Nobody would look in a mirror. Nothing would change. What had the teachers done *before* all this stuff happened? What had *anybody* done?

CHAPTER 10

C OLE WASN'T ABLE to talk with Peter during the day, but after school he caught up to his friend and gave him a big hug. "Who hurt you?" he asked.

Peter shook his head. "It doesn't m-m-matter."

"You and I need to have a talk," Cole said.

Peter shrugged as they headed away from the school grounds. For several long minutes neither of them spoke. Peter kept his head down and finally he muttered, "I did like you did. Every time I was picked on, I told the bullies I'd report whoever touched me. It worked until I w-w-went into the bathroom and somebody shut off the lights. Then a bunch of guys started hitting me and kicking me."

"Was it Keith and his friends?"

"It was dark and they never said anything when they were beating me up," Peter said. "I'd be really pissed if Keith was one of them after you helped him."

"Me, too," Cole agreed. "Are you okay now?"

"No, I'm not okay." Peter broke into tears. "I'm scared. Everything's messed up—I keep having nightmares and I can't think straight. My parents always argue over me, and I don't think people will ever quit picking on me."

Cole kicked angrily at a pinecone on the sidewalk. "I wish the whole school could be part of a Circle."

"They should line everybody up around the football field and make them hold hands," Peter said.

Cole stopped walking and stared at his friend.

"What's wrong?" Peter asked.

"Why *couldn't* the whole school gather around the football field?" Cole said. "Instead of a feather, we could pass a bullhorn because that's the only way everybody could hear."

"It wouldn't work 'cause most kids won't hold hands with anybody."

Cole thought a moment. "Some kids would think standing in a Circle was dumb. But they wouldn't have to join the Circle if they didn't want to."

"They could go sit in study hall instead," Peter said, looking up. "Do you really think it would work?"

"We'll never know unless we try. Tomorrow morning, let's meet early at school and talk to Ms. Kennedy."

"You t-t-tell her the idea?" Peter said. "I'm not so good at talking."

"I will," Cole said.

Peter looked at his watch. "Oh, c-c-crap, I gotta go. My parents are probably freaking 'cause I'm not home from school yet."

"Will they be mad at you?" Cole asked.

Peter smiled. "I'll just tell them you beat me up."

"Not funny," Cole said.

As planned, Cole and Peter met at the school half an hour early the next morning and went directly to the principal's office. "Can I help you?" she asked, her voice sounding tired and a little short.

"We have an idea," Cole said.

"I'm kind of busy this morning."

"So are we," Cole said. "This can't wait."

The principal motioned them briskly into her office. "How are you doing, Peter?"

"Things are all messed up," Peter said, sitting down.

She looked at Cole. "So what's so important?"

Cole didn't know where to begin so he just started talking, explaining their idea for a schoolwide Circle.

Ms. Kennedy listened, then studied both boys intently. "Wouldn't it be easier to just get everybody together in the gym and do the same thing? It would be—"

Peter interrupted. "People in a Circle have to look at each other."

Cole nodded. "Peter's right. Everybody feels like they're a part of a Circle—they're not just sitting behind somebody else in an audience."

Ms. Kennedy shook her head slowly. "I can't require students to attend something like that."

"Let the r-r-rest go sit in study hall," Peter said.

Almost pleading, Cole said, "Ms. Kennedy, you said it

yourself—all your changes don't mean anything if we don't change ourselves inside."

"You have this whole thing figured out, don't you?"

"Yup," Peter said. "We figured it out."

Ms. Kennedy rolled a pen back and forth in her fingers the way she had toyed with the feather in the Circle. "Tell you what . . . let me think about your idea for a few days."

"No," Cole said. "This has to be done right away while everybody is still thinking about Peter getting beat up and Trish's suicide. Garvey said that when the ground is torn up, that's when seeds need to be planted."

"Right now the ground is *really* messed up—it would work!" Peter exclaimed.

"I'll give your idea some thought, that's all I can promise," Ms. Kennedy answered. "Now, if you'll excuse me, I have a school to run."

The announcement by Ms. Kennedy came over the loudspeakers the following morning before the end of first period.

"Since our last assembly, some of you have come to me asking what you can do. Well, today each of you will have the chance to share your ideas. At nine o'clock, all teachers will bring their students out to the football field. We'll gather around the track in a big circle and talk. Any student not wanting to participate can report to study hall in the cafeteria."

Cole almost shouted with excitement.

★ ★ ★

Anticipation hung in the air as the students filed from the school, curious about why they were gathering around the football field instead of in the gym. Cole searched the crowd for Peter but couldn't find him.

Ms. Kennedy waited on the field inside the track, holding a bullhorn. "Everybody line up around the track in a single line," she directed. "Make a complete circle."

With the usual confusion that comes from asking any large group to do something simple, the students clumped in bunches. Some kids jostled to stand next to their best friend or refused to stand next to somebody they didn't like.

"Spread out," called Ms. Kennedy. "Form a single line around the track and face me."

When they finally did, Ms. Kennedy began. "Okay, everybody, listen up." The bullhorn sounded raspy, echoing across the field in the brisk morning air. "We have somebody here this morning who has agreed to come on very short notice and help you find ways to heal your school. I want to introduce Mrs. Holms, a trained mediator here in Minneapolis."

Cole recognized Mrs. Holms, the Keeper from his Circle.

"Good morning!" she began, speaking into the bullhorn. "I'm saddened by the reasons that bring us together today, but I'm encouraged that all of you are willing to gather like this to try and find solutions."

Cole glanced around the field, surprised to see how many had chosen to join the Circle. Kids rubbed at their arms and pushed their hands deep into their pockets to ward off the morning chill. Some were whispering and nudging each other, but most waited quietly. Keith stood between two younger students, not with his gang. He nodded to Cole.

"I must say this is the largest Circle I have ever been a part of," Mrs. Holms said. "But our size makes no difference. We will pass the bullhorn around the field and each of you will have the opportunity to voice your feelings if you wish. I ask only two things of you this morning. First, speak honestly from your heart. Second, respect whoever is speaking. If you can't respect others, you can't respect yourself. A school cannot heal without respect."

Two girls near Cole giggled. One boy hid a lit cigarette.

The Keeper spoke calmly through the bullhorn. "People always fear what they don't understand and destroy what they fear. Students, your ignorance and fear have let you focus on your differences. Prove today that you aren't afraid. I want everybody, including teachers, to reach out and join hands. Everyone form an unbroken Circle."

A murmur erupted around the track. Some students hesitated and tried to move quickly next to somebody else.

"Please, don't change positions," the Keeper said. "If students in the same school can't even hold hands, how do you expect countries to get along? It begins here."

When the human Circle was finally complete, the Keeper continued. "I'd like each of you to take a moment and think of something you have done in the last two weeks that showed intolerance. Some moment when you didn't allow somebody else to be different from you."

Everyone stood silently, some with closed eyes. In the distance, a siren wailed as the Keeper continued. "Okay, now I want each of you to think of what you could do, starting today, to encourage tolerance in your school."

"This is ridiculous," Cole heard one student complain. The boy left the Circle to join several others who were heading back inside.

The Keeper ignored the few who were leaving. "Okay, feel free to warm your hands in your jackets. I'm going to walk this bullhorn around the track twice. First, I want to hear your feelings about what's happened, and why you think we have such intolerance at this school. The second time around, we'll search for answers. But first let's share our hurt. Remember, nobody is required to speak, but we all have the obligation to listen."

The Keeper walked to the nearest student and offered him the bullhorn. Cole watched with anticipation, holding his breath.

The boy shook his head, embarrassed.

CHAPTER 11

THE KEEPER OFFERED the bullhorn to nearly a dozen students. With each refusal, Cole felt a sinking feeling grow in his gut. Finally, a tall blond girl found the courage to speak.

"What happened last week is only the tip of the iceberg," she began. "We all know the different gangs—the jocks, the cheerleaders, the nerds. Everybody belongs to some group and looks down on the others. We all share some blame for what happened."

"I agree," said the next girl in line. "I've hassled others myself and didn't think it was any big deal. But I guess it probably hurt them plenty."

Several more students refused to speak. The next student who accepted the bullhorn said, "Yeah, maybe a little hurt from a lot of students could cause somebody to commit suicide."

As the Keeper circled the field, everyone reacted differently. Some wiped away tears; others stood quietly with their eyes closed. Some stared sullenly at the ground. "I don't know what to do," one boy admitted. "I can't stop the bullies, drugs, and gangs. I'm afraid to even come to school some days."

Cole looked around the big Circle, no longer seeing the smirking, elbowing, or laughing. Maybe the Circle was working.

The sun started to warm the air as the Keeper worked her way around the field. Cole chose not to speak the first time she passed. Hopefully he would have the guts to speak when she asked for solutions. An idea had been prying at him all morning.

After nearly an hour, the Keeper walked to the center of the field. "I've so appreciated the honesty and respect with which you've spoken this morning," she said. "Now I want all of you to think of this school as something you own. Think of it as a body, and yourself as a part of it. What can you personally do now to heal your body? What changes can you each make to keep the tragedies of last week from repeating themselves?" Once again the Keeper walked around the Circle, offering the bullhorn to each student.

"We all have to let bullies know they aren't cool," said one girl.

"We have to quit putting each other down," said another.

Cole remembered the next student who spoke, from having picked on him years earlier. The boy said, "Teachers have the right to teach and students have the right to learn. Nobody has the right to take away those rights. Nobody."

One of the cheerleaders suggested, "Maybe we can have a mentoring program where kids who are flunking a subject can be helped by ones that are acing the course. We could share our strengths."

A senior boy shouted through the bullhorn, "Our differences should be our strength, not why we fight."

Students applauded some suggestions and murmured disagreement at others as the bullhorn circled the field. Cole noticed that Keith turned down both his chances to speak.

As the Keeper approached the second time, Cole shifted nervously. Maybe he should skip sharing his idea—everybody would probably think it was silly. Still, he found himself holding his hand out. The Keeper smiled, recognizing him as she handed him the bullhorn. It was too late to back down now.

"Most of you know who I am," Cole began awkwardly. "I've done things that I will always be ashamed of at this school. I also know that some of you still hate me—I'm sorry for that. I don't want this Circle to end today with just a bunch of talk. We need to do something big to show how serious we are about changing."

Cole licked at his dry lips and continued. "When I was on the island in Alaska, I almost died. But a bear called a Spirit Bear came to me like a dream and taught me who I was inside. The Spirit Bear was my inner strength. I learned that if a person's spirit dies, life isn't worth living." Cole drew in a quick breath. "We are the Minneapolis Central Bulldogs—that is our mascot. But if our greatest strength comes from the spirit inside each of us, why do we use a snarling dog to show our strength?

"I want to suggest that we change our mascot from a snarling bulldog to a Spirit Bear to show our commitment to changing ourselves."

Murmurs and whispering spread around the Circle.

The Keeper took the bullhorn and said, "Students, all suggestions you offer here today will be noted down. Later, *you* will decide which changes you want for yourself or for your school. The mascot idea will be added to the list."

Half an hour later, the Keeper ended the Circle the same way she had begun nearly two hours earlier, by asking everybody to join hands. This time, few students hesitated. Some even hugged each other.

"Thank you for showing your inner strength today," the Keeper said. Then she added with a chuckle, "Thanks for connecting with your own Spirit Bears. I want to remind each of you as you leave this field that any words spoken today are simply wasted sounds unless you do something about them. Your real test will come after you return inside. Then we'll see how committed you truly are to change. I'd wish you good luck but this has nothing to do with luck. This is all about choices, consequences, and commitment. I do wish each of you strength."

Cole breathed a huge sigh of relief as the students broke from the Circle and headed back toward the school for lunch. When he glanced around for Peter, Cole saw something else instead—the old homeless man standing outside the chain-link fence at the far end of the field.

Even from a distance, the familiar hunched shoulders, white blanket, and shopping cart were unmistakable. Cole wondered how long the old bum had been watching.

Back in class, most teachers skipped the day's planned lessons and talked instead about making changes. It pleased Cole that nobody had laughed at his suggestion of changing the mascot to a Spirit Bear. Maybe students *could* imagine the possibility of changing their own destinies.

After school, Peter asked Cole, "How come you didn't tell me about your idea of changing the mascot earlier? Aren't we friends?"

Cole gave Peter a quick one-armed hug. "Of course we're friends. I just wasn't sure a Spirit Bear mascot was such a good idea. That's why."

"Shoot, that's all anybody talked about in my classes the rest of the day."

"Hey," Cole asked, "did you see that old guy standing by the fence?"

Peter nodded. "I was down at that end. He just showed up suddenly . . . then he stood and stared at me. It was kinda spooky."

Cole shrugged. "Probably curious why so many students had gathered around the football field."

"He was shivering."

"All he ever wears is that thin white rag of a blanket," Cole said.

"Maybe I should give him the at.óow. That's warmer."

"You can't give him the at.óow!" Cole said, thinking

about the colorful blanket Garvey had given him. The at.óow had helped him to learn respect for his past before he'd given it to Peter. "Let's go to the Salvation Army store and buy him a good warm blanket instead."

"Is that what you would want for yourself?" Peter asked. "A used b–b–blanket from the Salvation Army?"

"Garvey gave me the at.óow as a special gift," Cole argued. "That thing is like a family treasure."

Peter grew quiet.

"I'm not trying to hurt your feelings. But you can't just give the at.óow to some bum. Garvey trusted me, and that's the same reason I gave it to you."

Peter nodded. "The at.óow *is* special to me, and maybe I trust the old man."

"We don't even know him."

"Because we haven't *tried* to know him," Peter said. "Besides, how well did Garvey know you? How well do you really know me?"

Cole didn't like that they were arguing. "Maybe we could just walk down to the Salvation Army and see if they have any blankets."

"Whatever," Peter mumbled.

"Do you need to let your parents know?"

"Let them look for me," Peter said, starting down the street toward the Salvation Army store a mile away.

"I'm not mad," Cole said.

"Neither am I," Peter said, hobbling faster.

It took almost a half hour to reach the big white building. Neither of them spoke until they pushed through the front doors. A tired-looking checkout lady directed them behind the women's dresses to a big shelf filled with blankets.

"There, now you can have your choice," Cole said to Peter. "I'll split the cost of buying one and we'll give it to the old bum as a gift from both of us."

Silently Peter examined each blanket on the shelf. When he finished looking at the last one, Cole asked, "So what do you think?"

"I don't like any of them," Peter said.

"There's about a half million of them—how can you not like any of them? We're looking for something to keep a homeless bum warm, not something to win a contest."

"I said I didn't like them," Peter snapped, heading toward the front entrance.

Cole knew not to argue the point anymore.

"Let's go past the abandoned building," Peter said.

"Why?"

"I want to meet the old guy."

"No way," Cole said. "He's probably a drug addict or an ex-convict."

"Like you," Peter shot back.

Cole gave up. "Do whatever you want with the at.óow. It's yours."

"I know that," Peter said.

They walked in silence until Peter stopped suddenly and pointed. Ahead of them was the homeless man struggling to push his grocery cart down the sidewalk. He had a tree stump balanced awkwardly across the top of the basket.

The sides of the cart bowed under the weight. Peter angled across the street, directly toward the homeless man.

Cole followed reluctantly.

The grizzled old man didn't notice them at first as he grunted and strained to keep the cart moving.

"What's he doing?" Cole whispered, approaching to within twenty feet.

"Go ask him."

"This was your idea," Cole said.

Peter hesitated, slowing almost to a halt.

Suddenly the homeless bum stopped and turned to stare at them. Cole and Peter froze in their tracks. Cole was about to run when Peter asked, "Do you n-n-need help pushing that thing?"

The man squinted at them. His stringy combed hair hung to his shoulders. Only a knotted rope around his waist kept his pants from falling down. Slowly his gaze softened as he recognized them. Then he smiled and shook his head before turning back to his cart. Not pressing their luck, Cole and Peter headed for home.

Cole felt bad. This was the first time since being on the island that he and Peter had really argued. Before splitting up, he said, "Peter, I'm sorry for things I said today. I just thought it was kind of dumb to give the at.óow to a homeless guy."

"Isn't it kind of d-d-dumb trying to make friends with Keith and changing the mascot name to Spirit Bear?"

Cole grinned. "Not any dumber than thinking the whole school should meet in a Circle."

CHAPTER 12

ALL WEEKEND COLE wondered if the Circle would change things.

On Monday morning, an uneasy calm hung in the air as teachers and police patrolled the halls. Metal detectors still guarded each entrance. A list of eighteen suggestions made during the Circle was handed out during first period.

Cole looked down the list and smiled. Someone had suggested that kids determine and enforce the dress code. Another suggestion was to start a newspaper so kids could be heard. He liked the suggestion of students meeting to help solve problems like vandalism and bullying. One idea Cole liked almost as much as his own was the suggestion that teachers be graded by students. Some teachers were a joke and had no clue how to teach. They demanded respect instead of earning it. Some classes were so boring, kids deserved extra credit for staying awake.

The problem was that you couldn't flunk a teacher. Cole had heard it was nearly impossible to fire teachers once they'd taught for a while. And if teachers couldn't be fired, what good would it do to flunk them? Maybe just posting the teachers' grades would help. But they would never allow that either. Some teachers were like bullies—they could dish it out but they couldn't take it.

Cole glanced one more time over the list. Hopefully, changing the mascot from a bulldog to a Spirit Bear wasn't just a dumb idea.

That afternoon, Ms. Kennedy called another assembly. She spoke bluntly. "I heard a lot of big ideas Friday," she said. "Now it's time to put up or shut up." She held up the list. "Each suggestion has a number." She pointed out to the gym floor, where eighteen teachers were each holding a large cardboard number. "Pick a change you want to see, and when I give the word, go in an orderly manner to that number. The teachers will help you organize and elect a student leader. Then it will be up to you personally to work with your team to come up with a concrete plan to try and make your favorite suggestion become a reality."

Ms. Kennedy examined the gym full of students. "This is all about change," she said. "Today we'll see how badly you want it. I'll fight to help you, but only if you fight, too." With that, students spilled from the bleachers to find their groups.

"I thought you said this was a dumb idea," Cole said, when Peter joined the others who wanted to change the mascot.

Peter grinned. "I had to come and see how dumb."

Cole looked around. Nearly two hundred students had gathered near his number. Theirs was the largest group. As smaller groups moved out of the gym, the mascot group remained behind in the bleachers with Mr. Brame, the band instructor.

"You have picked probably the hardest task," said Mr. Brame. "It's not easy changing a mascot. Besides financial costs, you'll need approval from the school district. That won't be easy, given the number of alumni who fondly remember their days here as Bulldogs. But, unless somebody has cold feet, let's get going. Are there any nominations for a group leader?"

A tenth-grade girl with a long ponytail said, "Because Cole Matthews met the Spirit Bear and made the suggestion, I nominate him."

The whole group responded with applause and agreement. Cole looked around desperately, but no additional nominations were made.

"Okay, then," said Mr. Brame. "If there are no further nominations, I propose that Cole Matthews be elected as leader of your committee to change the mascot from a bulldog to a Spirit Bear. All those in favor, say aye."

The whole group shouted, "Aye!"

Cole wanted to shout no! at the top of his lungs, but this *had* been his idea.

Mr. Brame turned to Cole. "It looks like you're now the leader. I'm turning it over to you."

Cole panicked as the bleacher full of students turned

and stared at him. He stood up and worked his way down to the floor of the gym, where he could face the whole group. "Uh, I've never done anything like this before," he stammered, looking around. "I'll do my best, and if nobody minds, I'd like to appoint Peter Driscal as my assistant. He has seen the Spirit Bear, too."

Peter blinked with surprise, then jumped to his feet and rushed down. He stood beside Cole with his shoulders squared.

Cole looked up into the bleachers and began. "Okay, how can we make this happen? Coming up with the idea was the easy part."

"The dumb part," whispered Peter.

As Cole waited for suggestions, Ms. Kennedy stopped by. "Do you mind if I make a short comment?" she asked.

"Uh, no, go ahead," Cole said.

Ms. Kennedy spoke loudly without a microphone. "Your group needs to prove that most of the students want to change the mascot, either with a vote or by signatures collected on a petition. I'll need that before I can submit it to the district office for consideration. Good luck!"

Cole had never organized people before—he had always been the screwup, the disrupter. Now it irritated him when kids chatted among themselves, making it hard for him to speak. Purposely he slowed his breathing and kept from getting angry.

"A few students think this is a dumb idea," Cole said, giving Peter a playful nudge. "Well, the thing that will make this idea work isn't if it's dumb or not but if we're all willing to make it happen. If anyone here isn't ready to work and fight to make this a reality, please join some other group."

Cole's challenge sparked excitement. Three eleventh graders raised their hands and volunteered to write a proposal letter explaining the reasons for wanting the mascot change. Another group of five decided they would do a rough cost estimate because that was something the principal and the school district would need. Cole worried. What if the cost of changing uniforms and signs, printing new stationery, having a new statue made, and painting a new mascot on the gym wall was too high? Everywhere Cole looked he saw growling bulldogs.

What surprised Cole as the meeting progressed was how many of the students were followers but willing to help if someone told them what to do. By the time the period ended, the group had a plan. Instead of putting the change up for a student vote they decided to gather signatures—this would allow more time to convince reluctant students. Getting enough signatures wouldn't be easy, but everybody promised to help.

As Cole left school that day with Peter, they stopped beside the bulldog statue.

"You two are wrecking our school!" shouted one of the jocks, walking by.

"You can't wreck something that's already wrecked!" Peter shouted back angrily.

"Hey, Peter, we're Spirit Bears," Cole reminded his friend. "Spirit Bears are strong, gentle, and kind."

Peter thought a moment. "You got mauled, so that proves they can get pissed off, too."

A few days later, Cole ran into Keith alone in the hallway. They both stopped and stood awkwardly, staring at each other. Cole broke the ice. "How are you?" he asked.

Keith shrugged. "Still sore."

"Did you sign up for something?"

"Yeah—the newspaper," Keith said.

"Do you like to write?"

Keith shifted his weight nervously from foot to foot. "I'm lucky to sign my name."

"We can use help changing the mascot," Cole said. "Maybe you could get some of your friends to sign the petition."

"I'll think about it," said Keith. "Most of my friends are losers."

"Hey, Keith," Cole asked bluntly. "Were you one of those who beat up Peter?"

Keith looked up at the clock on the wall. "I better get to class," he said, turning away.

Each day, Cole spent every spare minute with Peter and dozens of other students, circulating petitions and coaxing signatures from anyone who could hold a pen. One day Keith showed up unexpectedly and joined them, but he avoided Peter.

Some students refused to sign the petition, which was their choice, but one eleventh-grade football player threw the petition on the floor and gave Cole the finger. "I don't give a rat's butt what happens to this school," he said with a smirk.

"You don't care about your future 'cause you don't care about yourself," Cole answered calmly, picking up the sheets of paper. Before going to the island, he would have beat the jock silly.

When the last signature was collected, more than ninety percent of the students had signed. Armed with the petition, a cost estimate, and a letter stating the reasons for wanting a new mascot, Cole went to see Ms. Kennedy.

"I'm not sure how much good this will do," she said, thumbing through the petition.

"Then why did we do all this work?" Cole said sharply.

"I'll forward this with my recommendation to the district office," she said. But to Cole it seemed like she had hardly glanced at the papers.

While they waited for an answer from the district office, some members of Cole's group brought pictures of Spirit Bears to school, arguing over which would look best as a mascot painted on the gym wall. A few of the cheerleaders worked on new cheers using the Spirit Bear instead of the bulldog.

Cole wished Ms. Kennedy had been more encouraging. What if the plan wasn't approved? What then? Cole knew that many adults looked at change as a threat.

Each day after school, Cole spent time with Peter, whose moods were more volatile since he'd been beaten up. Cole let him vent, imagining how he must be feeling.

One warm but blustery October afternoon, they walked down to the park. Cole beat sticks together like a drum while Peter tried to dance the way he had on the island. After spinning for several minutes in circles under the trees with his arms spread like an eagle, Peter stopped suddenly. "On the island, this was okay," he said. "But here I feel like a dork." He motioned toward several people who stood watching them with amused expressions.

Cole had to agree. Nothing was the same here, but he did feel he was starting to find a calm place deep inside himself where he could go when school and the city piled up on him. He hoped Peter was finding that place, too.

The sound of thunder caught their attention. "It's looking like rain," Cole said, glancing up at the dark clouds gathering overhead. "The school is only a block away— let's go there."

They headed out immediately, but sheets of rain were falling by the time they reached the school. Soaking wet, they ducked inside the front door.

"What a bummer," said Peter.

Cole remembered Garvey's words, that each person's own reality was how they reacted to something and not what actually happened. Cole turned to Peter. "This isn't a bummer if we don't want it to be."

"What do you mean?" Peter said, shaking his wet head like a shaggy dog. "I'm soaked, and that sucks!"

"Only if we let it suck. I'll show you what I mean— follow me." With that, Cole dashed suddenly back out into the drenching downpour.

"What are you doing?" shouted Peter, hesitating at the doorway. "We don't have raincoats."

"It's a warm day, so staying dry or getting wet doesn't make any difference," Cole shouted. "I choose to be happy—that's my reality!"

"Okay!" Peter screamed, running into the deluge. "Take that, you dumb rain!" he shouted, chasing Cole around the parking lot.

For ten minutes they ran in circles, laughing and splashing their feet in the puddles. Finally, soaked to the bone, they ducked back inside. Ms. Kennedy met them in the doorway. "Mind telling me why you two are running in the rain and screaming like lunatics?" she asked.

"We're making our own reality," Peter announced.

Cole grinned. "We're proving that the rain can't wreck our day."

Ms. Kennedy shook her head. "You two are crazy." She looked at her watch. "I'm leaving. I'll give you two fools a ride home if you like."

"We're all wet," Cole said.

"That's okay—my old wreck has seen a lot worse than two wet maniacs."

As they followed Ms. Kennedy to her car, Peter suddenly stumbled on the curb and fell hard across the wet pavement.

"Are you okay?" Ms. Kennedy asked, rushing to his side.

Peter rolled over on the wet ground, grimacing and

holding his knee in pain. "I'll be okay," he groaned. "Dumb curb."

Cole smiled. "Peter, skinning your knee isn't reality. That's just what's going on outside your body. You can still be happy inside, remember."

Peter looked up. "It hurts, you jerk. That's my reality." Then, without warning, he kicked Cole hard in the shin.

"Ouch," said Cole, jumping backward. "Why did you do that?"

"Oh, that kick wasn't *your* reality," Peter mimicked. "You're just whining. Pretend it didn't happen."

All three broke into laughter, and they kept laughing as Cole helped Peter to his feet and they crawled into Ms. Kennedy's blue station wagon.

CHAPTER 13

I T WAS ANOTHER week before any word came back on changing the mascot. Ms. Kennedy's voice sounded tired during the morning announcements. She ended by saying, "I'm sorry but the plan for a Spirit Bear mascot has been turned down by the district office. Thanks to all the students who worked so hard on that project."

Cole felt like he had been kicked in the gut. First, adults told students that they could make a difference and that they should be responsible. Then they refused change. How could they refuse something that so many students wanted and worked for? It wasn't fair.

"Maybe this request being turned down isn't our reality," Cole told Peter after school.

"I don't get this reality stuff," Peter admitted.

"Maybe having our idea turned down is just the first step," Cole said. "Maybe the most important step is how we react to that rejection. Do we lie down and give up or do we fight? Maybe that decides our true reality."

Peter looked puzzled.

"I'll show you," Cole said. "After school, we'll go back and talk to Ms. Kennedy."

"I'm sorry about the district's decision," Ms. Kennedy said plainly as they entered her office.

"How could they turn down our proposal?" Cole asked with frustration. "Over ninety percent of the students signed our petition. Haven't they heard of democracy?"

She looked at them over her glasses. "Haven't you heard of bureaucracy? They said the cost of changing sports and band uniforms would be prohibitive. They think the Minneapolis Central Bulldogs have a rich tradition that needs to be respected and preserved."

"Uh, yeah, like a tradition of failures, suicide, gangs, shootings, and drugs," Cole replied.

"The main reason," Ms. Kennedy said, "is probably all the parents out there who once attended Minneapolis Central. They still have fond memories of being Bulldogs."

"That was their lives. What's important right now is *our* lives."

Ms. Kennedy threw her hands up. "They've made up their minds."

"And so have we," Cole said stubbornly.

Ms. Kennedy shrugged. "I suppose you could take it before the school board, but they usually follow the rec-ommendation of the district office." She stood and looked at her calendar. "They meet twice a month—next meeting is this Wednesday evening, upstairs at the district office. Every meeting allows time for public comments."

"I'll do that," Cole said, "but only if you're serious about helping us fight this. Otherwise we're wasting our time."

Ms. Kennedy leaned back. "This school has made some real progress since the Circle, but appealing the district's decision could open up a real can of worms for me."

"They're the ones who opened the can of worms by turning down our request," Cole said. He smiled. "Besides, what's more important, us or your job?"

That night Cole called Garvey. "Can you believe they turned us down when ninety percent of the students wanted the change?"

"That's why I don't like dealing with bureaucrats," Garvey said. "Just remember, real change seldom happens overnight."

"I just want it to happen in my lifetime."

"Then make it happen."

"But how?" Cole asked. Before Garvey could answer, Cole added, "I know—I'll think of something."

"You will," Garvey answered.

Nervous, Cole attended Wednesday night's school board meeting along with Peter. Several other students joined them, including Keith. Keith still acted funny around Peter.

Cole rehearsed what he planned to say in his mind, fearing he would open his mouth and nothing would come out but gibberish. He grew even more afraid when the board members started in with all their proper legal mumbo jumbo. Everything was proclamations, nominations, proposals, addendums, agendas, amendments, and motions. It was like a meeting of Congress.

Cole had the greatest urge to just leave and forget the whole stupid thing. Why should he care? Ms. Kennedy didn't. But too many students had joined him. He couldn't back out. Cole forced in deep breaths to keep from freaking. Finally the board chairman, a short balding man, announced that the meeting was open for public comments.

Cole raised his hand.

The chairman motioned toward the microphone at the front of the room and said, "Please step forward and state your name and address for the record and what it is you wish to comment about."

Cole wiped his sweaty palms on his jeans as he walked to the front of the room. There were nine board members and nearly fifty people attending the meeting. Cole swallowed, then stated his name and address. Why did they need his address? Were they going to publish this in the paper or turn it over to the police?

Briefly Cole told them who he was and what he had experienced on the island—something he suspected they already knew. "The Circle is what helped me," he said. "And that is why we had a Circle at school."

"Yes, I've heard about you and Alaska, and I also heard about your school's Circle," the chairman said. "But what is your request or comment tonight?"

"Well, the Circle is why I'm here," Cole said. "We need your help. Why is our mascot a growling bulldog if real strength comes from inside ourselves?" He paused. "The Spirit Bear showed me my inner strength. To show that we want real change, we want to change our mascot and team name to the Minneapolis Central Spirit Bears." Cole walked up and handed over the petition and cost estimates. "We've collected these—over ninety percent of the students agree this is what they want."

"It sounds good, but this type of request needs to be submitted to the district office," the Chairman said, glancing over the papers.

"We did that," Cole said. "And they turned it down—they said it would be too expensive."

"Have you considered that aspect?" another board member asked.

Cole nodded. "You have the rough estimates of cost with the petition, but the real costs are when students fail or turn out to be losers."

Board members exchanged glances as the chairman handed the paperwork down the table. "We'll take this under consideration. If we think there is merit, we'll schedule it as an agenda item for discussion at our next meeting in two weeks." The man took his glasses off and set them on the table to end the conversation.

Cole looked around. "So that's it?"

The chairman nodded and smiled politely. "That's it." He looked past Cole into the audience. "Are there any other public comments?"

Feeling defeated by the board's curt reaction, Cole left the meeting with Peter and the other students. Outside, one of the kids mimicked the board members. "We'll discuss this later," he said in a Donald Duck voice.

Everybody laughed. "Yeah, I'll bet they'll discuss it," one student grumped. "I'll bet the petition is already in the garbage can."

Cole turned to Keith. "Thanks for coming tonight."

"Whatever," Keith said, not meeting Cole's eyes.

"Is something wrong?" Cole asked.

Keith turned to Peter. "Can we talk?" he asked.

Peter eyed him suspiciously. "You were one of the guys who beat me up, weren't you?"

Keith shook his head. "No, but I know who it was."

"Who?" Peter said.

"I can't rat on my friends."

"You can't or you won't?" Peter said, staring. He blinked as he fought back tears. "If you protect them, you're scum, too!" he shouted. Then he turned and ran.

Cole looked Keith hard in the eyes. "Peter's right. If that's the kind of friends you want, you're scum, too. I thought you were better than them."

Keith hung his head. "I could have stopped it, but I wasn't big enough. I told the guys later that what they did was chicken and I've quit hanging out with them. Can you talk to Peter for me and explain?"

"Explain what? That you were a jerk and not able to stand up to a bunch of losers?"

Keith allowed a smile. "That would be a good start."

"A good start would be for you to do what's right," Cole answered.

"You mean rat on them?"

"I mean, do what's right."

The rest of that week, other proposals made progress at school. One group started up the program that had honors students helping struggling ones. The new school newspaper, *Our Voice*, ran its first issue. The front-page article was about grading teachers. One kid wrote, "Colleges allow professors to be graded. Companies allow employees to grade supervisors. If teachers don't want to be graded by students, maybe we need to start a black market grading system where kids vote and the results are posted on an outside Web site." The article concluded, "If teachers don't need permission to teach poorly, then why do we need permission to grade them?"

Several teachers threatened to have the newspaper closed down because of the article, but Ms. Kennedy sided reluctantly with the students, saying, "I support the paper and a student's right of expression as long as they respect other viewpoints."

"Ms. Kennedy is destroying this school," Cole heard one teacher comment to another in the hallway. Ironically, the teacher was Cole's history teacher. She was boring.

CHAPTER 14

WHILE HE WAITED to hear from the school board, Cole decided to visit his father one last time. Indian summer made the days warm and lazy as Cole caught the bus downtown after school. Maybe his father had changed some.

He hadn't. "From now on you call me before dropping in," his father snapped. "I might be with a client."

"Or you might not want to see me," Cole said. "You never call or stop by."

His father rocked back in his chair. "I told you, your mother and I don't see eye to eye these days."

"Why, because she quit drinking and you didn't?"

"You watch your smart mouth! I already told you, your mother and I don't get along because she filed abuse charges, turned me in to Social Services, won custody of you, and took me to the cleaners in the divorce settlement. How many more reasons do you need?"

"Dad, you were hitting and hurting me, and you were drinking a lot. You shouldn't have custody of me because you refuse to get help."

"Oh, so now I'm the one who needs help?"

"It couldn't hurt."

"What's the real reason you're here?" his father asked. "Does your mother want more child support?"

Cole hesitated. "I'm here 'cause I still love you."

His father turned and opened a file cabinet to hide his face. His voice wavered. "In your book, I'm just one big screwup, aren't I?"

"Dad, I didn't say that."

His father's voice hardened. "Listen, why don't you just worry about yourself."

"At least I'm trying," Cole answered. When his father did not look up, Cole turned and walked quietly from the office. "I won't bother you again," he said, closing the door. Cole blinked back tears as he ran from the building out into the bright sunlight. Tears flooded his cheeks.

Later that week, Ms. Kennedy called Cole to her office. "It looks like the school board has put our mascot proposal on their agenda for next Wednesday evening," she announced, as if she were the one responsible.

Cole had been so sure the request would be denied, his thoughts scrambled. "So how do we get ready?" he asked.

"The same as before," Ms. Kennedy said. "State your case clearly. Anticipate the arguments or questions the board might have and be ready with answers. They already have your petition and cost estimates. Maybe get more students to show up."

"Why am I the one that has to do the speaking?"

Ms. Kennedy took off her glasses and set them on her desk. "I've read through your juvenile file and you've been quite the troublemaker," she said. "Tell me, when you broke into a store to steal, did that scare you?"

Embarrassed, Cole nodded. "Sure. I was afraid of getting caught."

"So why did you still do it?" Ms. Kennedy asked.

"I don't know . . . maybe it was a challenge. Maybe I was just angry."

Ms. Kennedy nodded. "Right now you're scared of speaking because you're afraid of failing—it would be like getting caught."

"That's different," Cole said.

She smiled. "You did a lot of gutsy things as a troublemaker, but you've done even more daring things to turn your life around. Peter told me about your visit to Keith in the hospital—that took a whole lot of courage."

"But I don't want to be the group's leader," Cole said.

"Leaders are born, and I suspect you're one of them. The students in your group need a leader." Ms. Kennedy looked Cole directly in the eyes. "You were afraid as a juvenile delinquent, but it didn't stop you. So don't let it stop you now from doing something good. Fear is just life telling you to be careful. Tell me, do you want to see the school mascot changed to a Spirit Bear?"

"Sure," Cole said. "That would be good."

"Okay, then quit questioning yourself—it's wasting your energy. Roll up your sleeves and go make it happen."

Cole stood to leave the office. At the door, he turned back and studied Ms. Kennedy. Maybe she did care. "Can I ask you a personal question?" he said.

"What's that?"

"Why aren't you afraid of the gangs hurting you?"

Ms. Kennedy hesitated, pursing her lips before answering. "My husband died a few years ago, of bone cancer."

"I'm sorry," said Cole.

"So am I," she replied. "We both fought his cancer for five years. Compared to cancer, somehow a bully doesn't seem so tough."

Cole spent the next few days preparing for the hearing. Each day, his team gathered after school. Because cost alone could spell failure, team members made a more complete list with everything from bids on new uniforms to the cost of changing the school stationery. Working with the art teacher, several team members prepared a sample Spirit Bear logo to show the board. "Who came up with the bulldog mascot anyway?" one kid complained. "The mutt looks like it wants to eat someone."

Cole tried to think of everything. "Find out how old the uniforms are, too," he told his group. "If they're really old, maybe they need replacing anyway. And this time we need more students to attend the hearing."

By Wednesday evening, Cole's guts were tied up in knots. Peter met him early and they walked the half mile to the district office together. "Do you think the board members will change their minds?" Peter asked.

"They better," Cole answered defiantly, "or we'll be a pain in their butts."

"Yeah, we'll be hemorrhoids."

Nearly one hundred people crowded the room as the chairman called the meeting to order. Cole glanced around. Keith had not come tonight, nor had he helped the group since the night he talked to Peter. A reporter from the local newspaper sat at one side taking notes. Cole also noticed a large number of parents attending—that could be good or bad depending on whose side they were on. Shortly after the meeting began, Ms. Kennedy slipped in and seated herself alone near the back.

As before, the meeting droned on and on with financial discussions, salary decisions, and policy reviews. Finally the chairman announced, "Now it's time to discuss the Spirit Bear issue. Mr. Matthews, would you begin by explaining the students' proposal?"

Cole struggled to stay calm as he approached the microphone. Once again he spoke briefly of going to Alaska as banishment. He mentioned the suicide, vandalism, and beating that had occurred at school. Then he described the students' Circle around the football field and the proposal to change the mascot. "A Spirit Bear helped me understand myself during banishment. How can you ask us to be kind to each other if our mascot is a snarling bulldog?"

"I understand a Spirit Bear mauled you," a board member said.

"Only to protect himself. The Spirit Bear also let me touch him when I quit being angry. We want to change the mascot to a Spirit Bear because the students at Minneapolis Central have decided to turn their school around. Changing the mascot is our symbol of that effort. The Spirit Bear represents our own inner strength."

As soon as the chairman opened the floor for discussion, several parents approached the microphone. "Our teams have always been the Minneapolis Bulldogs," the first mother argued. "That's tradition."

"We have deep financial problems right now," the next parent said. "It's irresponsible to change mascots at this time. Changing band and sport uniforms alone would cost twenty or thirty thousand. That's too much money to spend so that somebody can have a cute little teddy bear on their jersey."

Cole forced deep breaths to keep from getting angry. Most of the adults here tonight had come to fight his proposal. What had he expected?

"Can anybody else address the cost issue?" a board member asked, looking toward the student section.

A quiet tenth-grader named Tina Olson approached the microphone. She sounded very businesslike when she said, "We checked and most of the uniforms at the school are almost twenty years old. I don't know anybody who wears clothes that old. Besides, we don't need to change the whole uniform to change the logo. All you need to do is change the jersey on the sport uniforms. With the band uniforms, we just have to make the Spirit Bear logo big enough to cover the bulldog."

Tina looked down at a piece of paper in her hand. "Our estimate is only four thousand three-hundred and eighty-two dollars and six cents. We're already planning fund-raisers. Changing mascots shouldn't cost the school anything." She returned to her seat as board members jotted down notes.

The next man to approach the microphone looked like a bulldog himself and grew even more belligerent. "I'm not going to stand here and let a bunch of impulsive children destroy our Bulldog tradition," the stocky man challenged. "What about the cost of a new mascot statue? You can't just whittle that out in shop class."

A shy boy Cole did not know stood and approached the microphone. "I'm new this year to Minneapolis Central," he said. "I guess I don't see the proud Bulldog tradition some parents have spoken about tonight. All I've seen are gangs and drugs. That's not much of a tradition."

When everybody had spoken, the chairman asked, "Are there any other comments before we vote on this issue?"

Ms. Kennedy stood and came forward. After stating her name and address, she said, "I hadn't intended to speak this evening, but I want this board to be aware of what will happen when they vote. If the students lose, I predict a dangerous explosion of emotions tomorrow—students will think they weren't given a fair hearing and their voices didn't count. Likewise, if the students win, I think much of the booster support we enjoy will be at risk."

Board members nodded as Ms. Kennedy spoke. Cole noticed the district superintendent in the audience. The silver-haired man listened intently but showed no emotion.

"Claims will be made that not all the facts were presented," Ms. Kennedy continued. "There will be accusations that board members themselves weren't well enough informed or that not enough notice was made for community comment before the vote. Many parents and students weren't even aware this issue would be voted on tonight.

"There could even be the risk of lawsuits. I guarantee, no matter how the board votes, there will be a fallout of anger and controversy. I suggest that your vote be deferred so you can hold a special meeting for the community. I think it would be prudent." Ms. Kennedy returned to her seat.

The board members spoke briefly among themselves, and then the chairman announced, "We agree with Ms. Kennedy. Considering the number of people here tonight, we will take final comments and vote on this issue at a special session in a larger meeting area. The date and location will be posted. A school's mascot is not to be taken lightly."

Cole noticed the local reporter scribbling furiously on her notepad. The chairman looked down at his paperwork and said, "The next item of business is district rezoning."

As Cole and Peter left the crowded room with the other students, the reporter approached Cole. "Do you really think changing the school mascot can change your school?" she asked.

Cole hesitated. "If we can change the mascot, maybe students will realize that they can control their own futures. This is all about change."

"Thanks." The reporter hastily waved down a couple of other students for interviews.

In the parking lot, Cole spotted Ms. Kennedy leaving and ran over to her. "How did this get to be such a big deal? All we want is to change a mascot," he complained. "We're not hurting anyone. Those parents make it sound like we're robbing a bank. We're just trying to change a picture on a wall."

"I thought you said a mascot was a lot more than that," Ms. Kennedy answered. "Otherwise you wouldn't have suggested the change. Would you be doing all this work for just a painting on a wall? Was that what you encountered on the island, a cute little teddy bear? Is that what changed your heart, a teddy bear?"

Cole shook his head. "Okay! Okay! You're right—it is a whole lot more and it means a whole lot more."

"Then start treating it that way," Ms. Kennedy said.

Cole eyed Ms. Kennedy. "I can't figure you out. When school started, you fought change. I figured you'd be gone in a week. Now I don't know what to think. Why did you ask for a special session? Now we have to go through this whole thing again."

Ms. Kennedy looked tired. "Because tonight you would have lost," she said.

CHAPTER 15

TWO DAYS LATER, the date for the special hearing was posted: Tuesday evening, November 7, in the high school gym. Suddenly, Cole became the center of attention. The newspaper interviewed him, and the local radio and television stations recorded segments for their evening news. Cole didn't like all the publicity. He wasn't always sure what to say except to encourage everyone to support changing the mascot. He found it worked better to speak from his heart instead of from his brain.

Keith kept to himself, not talking to Cole or helping the group anymore. Cole noticed he wasn't hanging around his old friends either.

Cole had never dreamed his proposal would turn into such a big deal. Students kept stopping him in the hallways to ask what he was going to do differently at the final hearing.

"I don't know," Cole answered each time.

He voiced his worries to Ms. Kennedy. "We've done all we can. We've put up posters all over town and in the school. The newspaper, radio stations, and television have helped, but I feel we should be doing more."

"There is one more thing," Ms. Kennedy said. "Make sure every student shows up."

Over the weekend, Cole's team spent every spare minute posting notices around town: HELP THE SPIRIT BEARS WIN and BE A SPIRIT BEAR, NOT A MUTT. Cole found himself glad when their football team lost their next game—it made it harder for parents to come to the hearing and brag about the school's proud Bulldog tradition.

Unable to sleep Sunday night, Cole crawled out onto the porch roof from his upstairs bedroom. He lay back and stared up at the sky. The darkness reminded him of the island. He thought about his struggle to change the mascot. He did want to make a difference in the world. He wanted to honor his ancestors and make them proud. But how? On the island, his choices had been few. It had been all about surviving, cooking, and cutting firewood. He'd eaten bugs and worms, even a mouse and his own puke. Here it was less simple. His opponent wasn't an injury, hunger, or weather. It was a school board and a whole community of parents and students.

On Monday, Ms. Kennedy offered to make an announcement to encourage attendance at the hearing.

"Thanks," Cole said, "but most students ignore announcements. Could you call everybody into the gym and ask them to attend? Like a pep rally?"

Ms. Kennedy shook her head. "I can't take any more time from teaching periods."

"Everybody talks big, but nobody wants to stick their neck out," Cole said.

"I hope you're not talking about me."

"If the shoe fits . . ."

Ms. Kennedy gave him a sharp look. "I'll make a deal with you, Mr. Matthews," she said, not smiling. "Tomorrow morning I'll call a full assembly in the gym, but you're the one who will do the talking."

"Why me?" he asked.

"Because everybody talks big but nobody wants to stick their neck out."

That night, Cole hardly slept a wink. He had fought Keith with his heart, but could he fight a school board and a gym full of angry parents with his heart? He dreamed of students laughing at him.

The next morning, true to her word, Ms. Kennedy called a full assembly. She quieted the students and then turned the microphone over to Cole. "Now it's up to you," she whispered.

Cole had written all that he wanted to say on a piece of paper, but when he looked at it now, the words blurred together. He paused to gather his thoughts and then folded the paper and just began speaking from his heart. "Tonight is the final hearing by the school board, here in this gym at seven o'clock. I'm not going to beg you to come. All I want to tell you is that there is a mess of adults who don't really respect you. They don't think you can make much of a difference. But this is *your* school now.

"We are making a difference with the things we're doing. We now have a newspaper, we have students helping other students study, and we have students helping to decide the dress code." Cole laughed. "The teachers still don't want us to grade them, but we are making a difference. We've already proved a lot of adults wrong. I know one thing—deep down, every one of you does care."

Cole paused the way he had seen Ms. Kennedy pause before saying something really important. Then he spoke quietly. "Tomorrow morning, each of you will get up and look in the mirror and know if you cared enough about yourself to help make a difference." Cole spoke louder. "Our school board and many parents don't think we care, so tonight let's all prove them wrong!"

It started with only a couple of shouts: "Go, Spirit Bears!" But slowly the chant grew louder and louder, spreading through the bleachers. "Go, Spirit Bears! Go, Spirit Bears! Go, Spirit Bears!"

Cole glanced at Ms. Kennedy sitting in the front row. She gave him a wink.

After school, Cole avoided Peter and returned home to spend time by himself. A little past six, he reminded his mother of the hearing but insisted on walking to the school alone. "I need time to think," he told her. He grabbed a quick sandwich and then headed out, walking the five blocks slowly. When he arrived, the parking lot was filling with cars. People crowded into the gym, excited as if they'd come for a basketball game. It scared Cole to think he was responsible for starting this whole thing. There was still a part of him that thought of himself as a loser.

On purpose, Cole sat alone in the back of the bleachers, looking out over the swelling crowd. To focus his mind, he closed his eyes and imagined a proud Spirit Bear walking toward him on the shoreline. The bear kept coming nearer and nearer as the time for the meeting approached.

Just before seven, board members arrived and found their places at a table set up on the basketball court. The gym was packed. At seven o'clock sharp, the chairman called the meeting to order. "Tonight is the final hearing on the proposal to change the proud Minneapolis Central Bulldog mascot to a Spirit Bear. The board calls Cole Matthews as the students' representative to explain the proposal."

Cole worked his way out onto the floor. Proud Bulldog mascot, my foot, he thought, stepping up to the microphone. Already the board was showing their bias. Coughs and whispers sounded through the crowd as Cole introduced himself and explained everything the way he had during the hearing at the district office. Then he drew a deep breath and spoke from his heart. "Years ago, somebody chose a bulldog as a mascot. And maybe it was a good inspiration for them. But a mascot represents both who you are and what you strive to become.

"Today, this school is filled with gangs, drugs, and violence; there's discrimination and bigotry. Is that the Bulldog tradition many of you are so proud of? A lot of students and teachers have decided to try and change this, but to do that we have to think, act, and feel different. We need major change. A new mascot won't solve everything. But it will be a symbol of what we're trying to accomplish."

Cole glanced back at the board. "If we change the mascot, the Bulldog can still be a good thing in your memories. You determined your own futures—please allow us to do the same."

Cole returned to his seat.

With the microphone echoing, the chairman announced, "Because of the large number of people here this evening, we have time constraints. We will strictly limit comments to one minute each. We will form two lines. On the right will be those opposed to changing the mascot. On the left will be those in favor. We will alternate between rows."

Students and adults spilled from the bleachers to claim a place in one of the lines. A few kids joined the line opposing the change of mascot, but most in that line were adults. Likewise, several adults stood in the line favoring the change, but mostly that line was kids. It looked like a contest between the students and the adults.

The first to speak was a red-haired girl. She walked to the microphone and said, "I want our mascot to be a Spirit Bear because I want to change myself. This is the first time I've ever really cared about anything, and I hope I'm not wasting my time."

Next a man who looked like somebody's grandfather spoke angrily. "My life has never really amounted to much, but every game I attend, I know that win or lose, I'll always be a Bulldog. You can't simply vote that away. Besides, we can't afford something like this just because a few students think it's a cute idea."

One by one the students and adults took turns speaking. One teacher said, "Some of you ask the financial cost of changing the mascot. It might be substantial, but the real costs will be staggering if students don't learn they control their own futures. I would trade ten years of my salary to bring back Trish Edwards, the student who committed suicide. What is the beating of a student worth? What does drug addiction cost? If you want to talk about cost, talk about the real costs when you deny these students their dreams."

The next lady walked up from the opposition line. "I am personally opposed to changing the mascot," she said, "but after hearing these students speak from their hearts about changing and controlling their futures, I want to say this: The Bulldog was our identity and our future, but who are we to tell these students what their identities and their futures should be? This is their school now, not ours."

Loud cheers erupted from the students. The chairman banged his gavel to restore order.

With each speaker, emotions grew more volatile. The owner of a local lumberyard stood and said, "I will always remember my high school days as a Minneapolis Central Bulldog, but as a business person I support the future." He pointed to all the students. "You are the future, and you have spoken with your petition and by being here tonight. If we change the mascot, I pledge that Olson Lumber will match each dollar you raise to fund that change."

Students whistled and cheered as the chairman rapped his gavel again for quiet.

Two hours after it began, the public hearing phase ended. The board conferred and called Ms. Kennedy to the microphone. "Whatever changes we make here this evening· will affect the administration of your school," the chairman said. "For this reason, the board would like to ask you, as principal of Minneapolis Central High, to share your thoughts and conclusions."

Ms. Kennedy carried a piece of paper with her to the microphone but didn't look at it as she spoke. "It's getting late, so just a few quick thoughts," she said. "At the beginning of the year, this school was out of control. What our students needed was structure, purpose, self-control, pride, dignity, and self-determination.

"Sadly enough, instead of focusing on the students, as a new principal, I was more concerned with pleasing our superintendent, parents, teachers, and the school board. I asked students to be responsible but did little to provide a school free of fear and intimidation." She scanned the crowded bleachers before continuing. "I asked students to evaluate their lives and to change their behavior. I asked them to put it all on the line and bet their futures on what they believed."

She smiled sadly. "I really talked big, telling teachers

that what they do for the students must be more important than keeping their jobs. But I wasn't following my own advice. Tonight, that is going to change. The students have spoken and I support them."

She looked over at Cole and Peter. "There are two boys here who taught me more than I ever taught them. They taught me that we can't be good educators if we play it safe. We must risk everything, every day, if that's what it takes. My number one concern from the start should have been the students.

"With all due respect, the Bulldog no longer represents strength, courage, or respect in this school. It is simply a vandalized statue outside the school entrance and a snarling canine face on the wall of this gym."

Ms. Kennedy walked over to the chairman and handed him the paper from her hand, then returned to the microphone. "That is my resignation. If you deny these students their request to control their own futures and change their mascot to something more meaningful, then I respectfully ask the school board to accept my resignation as principal of Minneapolis Central High School."

A stunned silence blanketed the gym as Ms. Kennedy returned to the bleachers.

A single voice from the bleachers shouted, "Go, Spirit Bears."

Nervous laughter rippled over the crowd as another student shouted, "Go, Spirit Bears."

It began as it had earlier in the day with sporadic shouting that quickly became a chant: "Go, Spirit Bears!

Go, Spirit Bears! Go, Spirit Bears!"

Cole turned and looked around the gym. Both students and adults were beginning to stand and chant.

The chairman kept rapping his gavel on the table for silence, but the chant grew louder and louder, becoming a thunderous roar. "Go, Spirit Bears! Go, Spirit Bears!" Nearly the whole gym was now on its feet. Cole caught Ms. Kennedy's eye and she gave him a thumbs-up.

The chairman quit trying to restore order. With the deafening chant echoing back and forth across the gym, each board member voted on a paper ballot and handed it to the chairman.

Deliberately he counted the votes.

CHAPTER 16

C OLE HELD HIS breath. The chairman rapped the gavel hard and pulled the microphone closer to his mouth. The chanting of "Go, Spirit Bears!" faded away reluctantly, leaving a charged and brittle silence.

"A two thirds majority vote is needed for the passage of this proposal," the chairman announced. "Tonight's vote is seven in favor and two opposed."

Cole had never liked math much, and for a split second he scrambled to think if seven of nine votes was a two thirds majority. The thunderous applause erased any doubt.

"Details of this change will be worked out in the coming months," the chairman added, speaking loudly to be heard above the applause and whistling. Then he held up Ms. Kennedy's resignation and said, "I'm glad to be able to do this." He ripped it in half. "Also, let me be the first to officially say, Go, Spirit Bears!"

The auditorium erupted again with, "Go, Spirit Bears!

Go, Spirit Bears! Go, Spirit Bears!"

Cole couldn't believe this was all happening—was it real? He remembered feeling this same way when he recovered consciousness in the boat after the mauling—he had waited to wake up from a dream. But being rescued on the island had been no dream. Nor was tonight.

Students and adults mobbed Cole, thanking him, congratulating him, shaking his hand, and slapping him on the back. Peter ran up, jumping and shouting and yelling, "We did it! We did it!"

Cole gave him a big hug, lifting him off his feet and swinging him in a full circle. "Yes, we did it," he shouted back. Cameras flashed, and everywhere people kept clapping.

When Cole quit swinging Peter, he noticed Keith beside them. Keith extended his hand to Peter. "I'm really sorry," he shouted. "I've told Ms. Kennedy who hurt you."

"You ratted?" Peter asked, showing his surprise.

Keith shook his head. "You can't rat on rats," he said. "It's what I should have done from the start." He kept his hand extended.

Still Peter hesitated.

It was hard to hear above the bedlam of noise. "Maybe change starts by forgiving!" Cole shouted to Peter.

Slowly Peter reached and shook Keith's hand.

"Go, Spirit Bears!" Cole shouted, cuffing them both on the shoulders.

Ms. Kennedy came up and gave Cole a big hug. "You and Peter created a new reality for everyone tonight," she said.

"With your help," Cole added. "I can't believe you offered your resignation."

She smiled. "We all had to put everything on the line. Just know I'm proud of you. And I'm proud of our school."

"Cole Matthews!" shouted a local television reporter, his camera rolling. "What do you think of what happened here tonight?"

"We did it!" was all Cole could respond. "We did it!"

One by one board members stopped to offer congratulations before leaving. As students kept shaking his hand, Cole's gaze swept out over the thinning crowd filing from the gym. One single figure caught his attention. Stopped against the moving crowd, looking back at him, stood his own father. For a split second their eyes met.

"Excuse me," Cole interrupted. "Excuse me, I'll be right back." But even as Cole started across the gym floor, his father turned and disappeared into the departing crowd. Cole searched frantically, running outside, but couldn't find him. Slowly he returned to the gym.

"Where did you go?" his mother asked.

"Nowhere," Cole said. "Just tried to catch an old friend."

Peter stood beside his smiling parents, still shouting "We did it! We did it!"

Garvey walked up to Cole. "I never knew you were such an eloquent speaker," he joked. "You beat them with your heart, your head, and your mouth."

"Thanks for all your help," Cole said.

Garvey cupped his hand and shouted into Cole's ear,

"Your father was here tonight and asked me if I thought a Circle could help an adult."

"What did you say?"

"I told him yes, if he wanted the change."

"Is that all he said?"

"Hey, it's a start."

Cole's mother stepped in and hugged Cole. "I'm so very proud of you," she said. "Do you need a ride home?"

Cole looked over at Peter. "I know it's late but I'd love it if we could go out for ice cream to celebrate."

Cole's mother nodded, turning to Mr. and Mrs. Driscal. "Do you mind if Peter joins us?"

Peter's father approached Cole and extended his hand for a firm shake. "I never thought I would see the day when I said this to the boy who hurt my son, but tonight I am very proud of you both. Can we join you? The ice cream is on me."

Cole nodded. "Can you come, too?" he asked Garvey.

"It would be an honor," Garvey replied.

Cole smiled in disbelief as he looked up at the snarling bulldog mascot on the gym wall. It no longer seemed so fierce.

The next day, Ms. Kennedy agreed that they needed to take down the bulldog statue and change the gym-wall mascot immediately. "I'll have the art department start right on it," she promised. "It may take a little longer to replace the bulldog statue with a Spirit Bear—that's something we want to make sure is done right."

Cole and Peter agreed.

At noon, students gathered to help paint over the old bulldog. Everyone cheered when the stroke of a paintbrush covered the last of the fierce mascot.

"Go, Spirit Bears," the students chanted.

Cole stood watching. Emotion blurred his vision and he kept swallowing. When he had carried the ancestor rock on the island, it represented all the generations of ancestors that had lived before him. If he squandered his life, he wasted their legacy. Now Cole realized that the legacy being created at this moment, here in this gym, was part of what he would pass on to a new generation.

By Friday, the art teacher and her students had outlined a Spirit Bear on the gym wall. Fourth period, Cole sat at his desk in history class, bored. Glancing out the window, he noticed snowflakes swirling around. All fall, the weather had been mild with unseasonably warm temperatures, but now a bitter wind kicked up out of the north and drove snow sideways past the windowpanes.

When school let out that afternoon, Cole met Peter by the lockers. "Did you see the snow?" Peter asked.

"Yeah, winter's here."

"Hey, have you seen the old homeless guy around?" Peter asked.

Cole shook his head. "Not since we saw him pushing that old pine stump in his cart. Why?"

"I'm going to take him the at.óow after school," Peter said. "He needs it to stay warm."

Cole didn't argue. Giving Peter the colorful blanket on the island had been part of his own healing—it showed he was capable of trust. Now, giving it away was also important to Peter.

"You don't mind, do you?" Peter asked.

"Would it make any difference if I did?"

"No."

"Then why did you ask me?"

"'Cause I wanted you to help me give it to him," Peter admitted.

"I thought you trusted the old guy—that's why you give somebody the at.óow."

"I do," said Peter. "But I thought you might want to come along because we're friends."

Cole smiled and nodded. "For sure."

Filled with anticipation, they headed for Peter's house to pick up the blanket. Neither had worn gloves to school, and their fingers and cheeks were numbed by the bitter, gusting wind. They zipped their jackets up and ducked their heads to protect their ears.

At Peter's house, Cole waited inside the entry as Peter ran up to his room for the at.óow and also a flashlight.

When Peter returned, the sight of the brightly colored blanket flooded Cole's mind with memories and emotions. He unfolded the at.óow carefully and wrapped it around his shoulders. Eyes closed, he buried his face in the soft wool and pretended that he was letting all his own ancestors wrap their lives around his for a moment. He felt their presence and their protection.

"Hello, Planet Earth to Cole," Peter said.

Cole opened his eyes and refolded the blanket. "Okay, let's do it."

Without talking, Peter and Cole walked to the old building. "Do you think he's in there?" Peter asked, his breath showing in the cold air.

"In weather like this, where else could he be?"

Cautiously, both boys slipped between the broken front doors. The grocery cart was gone. Peter snapped on his flashlight at the top of the stairwell. "Hey, mister!" he called. "W-w-we brought you something."

Cole called out, "Hello, anybody down there?"

Their voices echoed in the damp and dark stairwell.

"Let's just go down and leave it for him," Cole said.

"But then I can't explain to him how special and important the at.óow is," Peter argued.

"You want to come back?"

"I don't know," Peter said, starting tentatively down the steps. He probed the light into the darkness.

Cole followed. "Let me see the flashlight," he said, when they reached the bottom. He shined it into the corner where the old bum lived, but nothing made sense—everything was gone.

There was no mattress, no cardboard box for a table, nothing. Only wood shavings. The whole floor was covered with fresh wood shavings. Cole shined the light around the empty room. There was simply nothing. The homeless man had vanished with no sign he had ever been there. Cobwebs hung from the walls and ceiling, and dust covered the floor where the mattress had been.

"Where d-d-did he go?" Peter asked.

"Maybe he was never here," Cole said.

"What do you mean he was never here? We saw him. Let me see the light again." Peter grabbed the flashlight. Almost frantically, he flashed the beam around the room, searching for any sign of the old man.

That was when they spotted it.

Both boys gasped as Peter steadied the beam of light on a big object sitting in the far corner.

"It's a bear," Cole whispered.

"A Spirit Bear," Peter answered.

Surrounded by the wood shavings stood a magnificent white bear. It looked as if it had been carved from pine, and every detail down to the claws and eyes looked alive. Over four feet tall, the bear had a paw raised and head tilted to one side. It stared forward as if gazing into the future. When the light shined on its face, Cole saw gentleness, kindness, and strength.

Cole and Peter stood speechless for a moment.

"Wh-wh-why did he carve that?" Peter finally asked.

"To replace the bulldog statue," Cole ventured.

"But how did he know we needed it?"

Cole shrugged. "There's a lot of stuff we don't under-stand. Why does anything happen? Why did the Spirit Bear in Alaska keep following us?"

Peter held up the at.óow. "And what do I do with this now?"

"If this bear is displayed inside the school, maybe you

can spread the at.óow underneath for every student to see."

"To remind us of our ancestors?" Peter asked.

Cole nodded and whispered reverently, "And to remind us that we are each important and a part of the Circle."

Without speaking, they lifted the old man's gift. Balancing its weight between them, Peter and Cole carried the Spirit Bear up the dark stairs, through the doors, and out into their world.